D0843335

■

moshi moshi

■

Moshi Moshi

. . .

Banana Yoshimoto

translated by
Asa Yoneda

COUNTERPOINT
BERKELEY

Westhampton Free Library
7 Library Avenue
Westhampton Beach, NY 11978

Moshi Moshi Shimokitazawa by Banana Yoshimoto

Copyright © 2010 by Banana Yoshimoto

Japanese original edition published by The Mainichi Newspapers
English Translation rights arranged with Banana Yoshimoto
through ZIPANGO, S.L. and Michael Kevin Staley

Counterpoint Edition 2016

All rights reserved under International and Pan-American Copyright
Conventions. No part of this book may be used or reproduced in any
manner whatsoever without written permission from the publisher, except
in the case of brief quotations embodied in critical articles and reviews.

This book is a work of fiction. Names, characters, places, and incidents
either are products of the author's imagination or are used fictitiously.
Any resemblance to actual events or locales or persons, living or dead,
is entirely coincidental.

Library of Congress Cataloging-in-Publication Data is Available

Interior design by Domini Dragoone
Illustrations by Mai Ohno

ISBN 978-1-61902-786-2

COUNTERPOINT
2560 Ninth Street, Suite 318
Berkeley, CA 94710
www.counterpointpress.com

Printed in the United States of America
Distributed by Publishers Group West

10 9 8 7 6 5 4 3 2 1

moshi moshi

■ ■ ■

THE NEIGHBORHOOD OF SHIMOKITAZAWA FEATURES IN A MOVIE called *Zawa Zawa Shimokitazawa* by one of my favorite directors, the late Jun Ichikawa.

When I still lived in my childhood home, I watched the movie over and over, late at night, alone, to try and give myself the courage to move there. I wanted to immerse myself in the area until I felt confident in my decision.

One scene shows the pianist Fujiko Hemming talking about the town. The image shows Fujiko walking and shopping in the covered market near the station, while her narration comes in as a voice-over.

"The clutter of streets and buildings, which seem to have been left to spread and grow without any thought—they sometimes appear very beautiful, like a bird eating a flower, or a cat jumping down gracefully from a height. I feel that what might seem at first sight to be carelessness and disorder in fact expresses the purest parts of our unconscious.

"When we start something new, at first it is very muddy, and clouded.

"But soon, it becomes a clear stream, whose flow conducts itself quietly, through spontaneous movements."

The very first time I watched that scene, I marveled at the truth in what she was saying and found tears rolling down my cheeks. After that, I watched it over and over, committing it to memory and storing up my courage.

What a comfort it was, I thought, to hear someone put into words something that you were on the verge of grasping.

I knew her beautiful words had only gained the intense significance they had on film—their power to sway people's hearts, lift their spirits, and ground their feet to the earth—as a result of the accumulation of the myriad things that had befallen Fujiko in her life up until that point.

I longed to have the same kind of effect, in my own way—to cast such a wonderful spell over people.

When I thought about this, late at night, alone, it used to give me a space in which I could breathe deeply, without which I doubt I could have survived.

My depression after losing Dad wasn't acute—the suffering was more like a gradual accumulation of body blows. I would be deeply sunken into it by the time I noticed, and then barely manage to lift my face to break the surface and come up for air. It was a cycle that started over again before I knew it.

I grew pedantic and over-logical, and my body seemed to have hardened and shrunk. Out of self-protection, I took to wallowing in my own thoughts even more than before.

Flowers and light, hope and excitement all suddenly seemed like things that were very distant from me, and I was trapped inside a deep, putrid, and bloody darkness. In it, only the ferocious power that lay deep inside my gut had meaning, and what was beautiful or light had no value at all.

Inside that darkness, I tried my best just to keep moving, keep breathing, and keep sight of what I could see.

Then, gradually, I started to see some light.

It wasn't *the* light.

The darkness was still there, still in service to that brutish, feral bloodiness.

I didn't understand the deeper meaning of what Fujiko had said until I'd gained enough breathing space to appreciate the beauty of that contrast.

I MOVED TO SHIMOKITAZAWA ABOUT a year after Dad got mixed up in a love murder-suicide in a forest in Ibaraki with a woman who'd apparently been a distant relative, whom neither my mom nor I had known anything about.

The woman had approached Dad for advice, and eventually—after they'd become involved—she had lured Dad into meeting with her, drugged his drink, and driven him out into an isolated forest, where he'd died from carbon monoxide poisoning from the charcoal briquettes she'd brought with her. Of course, the woman had died, too. The car had been sealed so it was airtight, and there was no reason to suspect any other crime.

Although the incident gave the impression of a suicide pact, Dad—for all intents and purposes—had been murdered.

I don't want to say a lot about the ins and outs of the sobering scenes that took place, or the practical decisions that had to be made, and all the things that Mom and I had to see and hear because of that.

There was so much that was too shocking and too difficult to take in, and I didn't have the chance to make sense of it all.

My memory of that time is patchy. Maybe there never will be a time when I'm able to look back on the whole of it. If life is a process of accumulating more and more things you simply can't bring yourself to make peace with, well, my feelings about this are vast and deep enough for an entire lifetime's worth of hang-ups.

Mom and I had been oblivious. We said to each other: *There've been a lot of overnight trips and coming home in the morning lately, do you think he's found someone? I don't think Dad's got the guts to abandon his family, but what shall we do if it comes to that? I guess we just have to carry on as usual, there's no use thinking too deeply about things. He'll probably come back when he's ready.* When the police called, we were totally blindsided.

We cried, we wailed, we acted out—for a while, we tried everything. Anything at all. Sometimes together, sometimes alone, sometimes supporting each other.

We blamed ourselves, too, for having accepted Dad's indiscretions as an inevitable part of the music business, and, out of a strange kind of considerateness and somewhat resignedly, having left him to his unfettered lifestyle in the belief that to look too deeply into it would be to risk breaking up the family.

Aside from when he was on tour, Dad made it a rule not to spend the night away from home, even if that meant getting back at dawn, and he kept every promise he made to Mom or me, no matter how small, writing them down in his diary or on the back of his hand. Even now, when I think of his hands, I see them in my mind's eye covered in notes.

Dad, who essentially stuck to his promises on anything we asked of him, from *Could you pick up some milk on your way home?* to *Let's go out and get dumplings together next week*, was a good father first and foremost, even before his professional identity as a musician. So Mom and I had become complacent.

And that was why, when he died like that—and even after the funeral—we were still so surprised that it took a long time to really feel that he was gone.

Since the woman had died, too, there was no justice to be brought, and it all blew over without any resolution, without our feelings having anywhere to go. There had been no point seeking out her family to sue them for damages, since they might even have been related to us in some way, and we hardly wanted to meet them, either.

And anyway, it seemed that the woman had been put up for adoption soon after she was born, and when she died it had been a long time since she'd run away from the family that had adopted her, so she effectively had no family. Even this was information that had come to us unbidden, which truthfully neither of us even wanted to know. So Mom and I took no action about this.

I didn't look closely at her body, but from what I saw in a photograph later, she was chillingly pale and beautiful, and put me in mind of a fox or a snake. That, too, came as a shock—that Dad had been taken in by that kind of trite seductiveness. I'm sure it must have been far harder for Mom to bear.

But life went on, even at times like this, and it was surprising how easy it was to keep going as though nothing had changed. I found it strange that I could walk down the street and appear normal, just like anyone else. That I could be in complete turmoil inside, and yet my reflection in a shop window could look the same as it ever had.

Around a year after Dad died, feeling like Mom had started to get back on her feet, I finally took steps toward starting my own life.

I'd gone to culinary school straight out of junior college. Since graduating, I'd been slowly looking for a job while helping out at friends' restaurants, but all of that had been put on hold by what happened. I'd even been talking with some friends from culinary school about starting up somewhere on our own, but that was out of the question now, and I was starting over again from scratch.

I left the condo that had been the family home and rented the upstairs of a building owned by the mother of a friend, right on Chazawa-Dori, the main thoroughfare in Shimokitazawa. My friend had lived there until she got married and moved to England, and I took it over straight away. The room was seven minutes' walk from Shimokitazawa Station.

Soon after that, I started my job at Les Liens, a bistro within eyeshot of my apartment, on the other side of Chazawa-Dori. It was a small restaurant and I pitched in everywhere I could help—in the kitchen, at the front of the house, behind the bar—and just like that, my days were busy and full.

Once the heavy, stifling air at home had finally started to lift, living on my own was exactly what I needed. I thought I'd finally be able to shake off what happened with Dad, and move on with my own life.

I was finally starting to be able to feel the joy in sitting down to a cup of tea, or just getting up in the morning. It was amazing what a difference a change in scenery made. I could wake up without my first thought being that Dad was gone. Back at the condo, it welled up every morning, all around the apartment like a hidden message, clouding my heart.

I had the entire second floor of the old house, which was enough space, but not huge. The layout was simple: two rooms that faced west, laid with tatami mats, and a narrow kitchen. In summer, the afternoon sun shone in so strongly that turning on the air conditioning hardly made a dent in the heat.

The bathroom was old, and the small tub was tiled, but the shower had been installed just before I moved in and was brand-new. The rooms always had the characteristic smell of old houses, and the straw mats were dry and faded. The cook stove was antique, and the circuit breakers would get tripped half the time I tried to use my toaster oven, let alone the hair dryer, which could only be switched on if all the lights were out. It was a period piece, which made all my friends marvel that this kind of place still existed.

Even so, since I was happy to save up as much money as I could, the size, the cheapness, and the proximity to work were nothing short of a godsend. My friend's mother was a live-out landlady, and had leased the first floor to a small vintage clothes shop and a cozy coffee shop with just a bar and no tables. The coffee wasn't good and the cookies were underbaked, so I never went in, but it was run by friendly young women who were always there during the day, and at night there was no one to complain if my footsteps were too loud, or my music, or if I ran the washing machine, which was a bonus.

BUT MY HAPPINESS WAS short-lived. One day, out of the blue, without much more than the clothes on her back, Mom moved in.

It was late one drizzly afternoon, at a point in the year when the sky felt much higher all of a sudden—as if summer, with its relentless sun, had suddenly loosened its grip. There was a chill in the wind, and I knew fall was about to set in.

I'd just worked the lunch service at Les Liens, and was relaxing back at my apartment during my break. I got a call from Mom, who said, "I'm actually in Shimokitazawa right now."

She came over often enough, so I said, "I'm at home. Drop by for a cup of tea?"

But then she showed up with several big shopping bags and a Birkin bag stuffed to bursting, and, like it was nothing out of the ordinary, said, "Yocchan, I just can't stand living at home all alone anymore. Do you mind if I stay with you? Just for a while?"

I definitely did mind, and it was all I could do not to look annoyed. I restrained myself because Mom had been going through a hard time, too. Both of us were still nursing a lot of clouded, murky feelings that we weren't yet able to put into words.

But I could hardly believe what she was saying. I was working all the time and mainly just needed a place to sleep at night, so the apartment was in no way comparable to the modern and spacious three-bedroom condo in Meguro that had been the family home. But it didn't seem to matter to Mom. I'd counted on making a fresh start here, and now that I'd settled in at the bistro, I was itching to finally start having the kind of fun you got to have when you lived alone. I was looking forward to falling in love, or just having friends over to chat with. *No way,* I thought.

"Why don't we go back to Meguro together? Let me come stay with you for a bit," I said.

But she said, "I know it's not Jiyugaoka's fault, but the apartment, the whole neighborhood, reminds me of Dad.

"I like Shimokitazawa; this is where I want to be. That apartment's just stifling. There's no life there. I finally realized just how much of a comfort it was for me, Yocchan, having you around."

The condo in Meguro, not far from Jiyugaoka, had been gifted to Mom and Dad by my paternal grandmother, on the occasion of their having a child—me. So it wasn't like there was rent to pay while there was no one living in it. There was just the service charge, plus the owners' association meetings, which were only about once a month provided you weren't in charge of something that year. There was no real reason it couldn't be left empty for a little while.

"I'm going to give it six months, and if I don't feel differently by then, I'll sell it," she said.

"In that case, why don't we at least find a slightly bigger place than this? We could afford it, together," I said.

"But that would make everything much too definite. It would be a major undertaking. It's not the time for that yet. We've got to go slowly just now, slow enough not to disturb a single mote of dust. Slowly, quietly, holding our breath. Making a big move just now would be disastrous," Mom said.

She had a habit of coming out with strangely convincing ideas at times like this.

"This is where I want to be. When I'm looking down at Chazawa-Dori from this window, I can sense things slowly fading back to normal. Yocchan, please, for real—can't you make believe I'm a friend of yours? Just pretend one of your girlfriends has had her heart broken and needs a place to stay for a little while," she said.

I was looking at the pattern on the indescribably garish T-shirt she was wearing. She'd probably bought it in the vintage clothing place downstairs, and worn it here straight out of the changing room. She'd really embraced the Shimokitazawa look; the way she was dressed, you'd never have guessed she was a woman of leisure, a Meguro Madame.

"I can't just pretend, 'for real' or no! Anyway, the situation's way more serious than a breakup. I need to think about it," I said.

"I don't care if I'm pathetic for needing your help; there's no way I can stay in Meguro with Dad gone, and never seeing your smile either, not right now. I just need a break so I can start to face things again," she said.

My head was spinning. I was suddenly being forced to reconsider everything about the life I'd been picturing for myself. Why should the two of us have to live together in this run-down apartment, as if we were in some shabby hotel far from home, when there was the well-appointed condo in Meguro? I mean, I'd moved into my friend's mom's place, whose only advantage was its location literally across the street from the bistro where I worked, specifically so I could save on rent and put some money aside.

Mom was saying she'd chip in, meaning she'd cover most of the rent, and probably do all the cleaning and laundry, too. I might as well have not left home! Careful to put it gently, I told her as much.

But she kind of let it slide, not really seeming to take in what I'd said. "Every single thing you're saying is so sensible! You have reasons, and it's all so logical and thought through," Mom said.

"Well, yes," I said. "I mean, of course! Isn't that how it works?"

She shook her head. "I just want to do something that makes no sense right now. I want to forget about having to be a responsible adult. Because marriage and life and so on are all just a series of sensible decisions and expectations, and don't you think your father must just have wanted to do something illogical for once, and ended up in over his head, and that's why he died how he did?

"I want to do illogical things, too. I know it can't be exactly like when I was younger, but now that you're grown and off my hands, I just want to pretend like I'm crashing with a friend for a little while, and forget about everything, and just start over."

The funny thing was, once I was able to listen with an open mind to the things she was saying, they didn't seem so misguided after all. Her words resonated with me in a way I didn't quite understand.

Dad had been a fairly well-known musician. He played keyboards in a band, but guys he knew would also get him into the studio to play on sessions they were laying down, or ask him to join their bands when they went on tour. He was always in demand, and made good money from it, too.

When he was invited to teach at music schools, he'd agree to do a one-off lecture or a master class, but he always said he wasn't interested in teaching music for a living—it was playing live that he loved. And he pretty much lived doing what he loved, so he was constantly on the road with one band or another, and in recent years our family unit had gradually disintegrated to the point where we only saw each other every once in a while, when we happened to be at the house at the same time.

Families went through different phases. Ours had reached a stage when our hearts had become a little distant while we spent time apart, and we'd been waiting for the balance to shift again and bring us back closer together, when—without our knowing—Dad had been stolen away. Mom, who'd had quite a sheltered upbringing, and me, being her daughter, had hardly a drop of worldly cunning between us, and hadn't been able to compete.

For his part, Dad had never been the most vivacious of people. He was prone to illness, and could be neurotic, and tended to give people the impression that it took him all his energy just to stay alive, even though he wasn't actually that fragile.

It might have been in the blood—specifically, my paternal grandmother's. She'd been well bred and never wanted for money, but had led an unhappy life. Her husband, my grandfather, who died while Dad was still young, had kept a mistress, and was rarely home. I only learned this after my grandmother died.

It gave me chills to think that I had some of this tragic blood in my veins, too. Dad looked calm and mature on the outside, but inside he acted as though he was still in college. The kind of man who'd link arms with his daughter whenever we went out together—a high-spirited, naïve, and anxious person at root. He didn't come across that way to other people, because he looked quite sweet and delicate, and was quiet, but he took things hard, and would rather have floated through life. He had a kind of naïvete that let him think that things would turn out all right. That childlike quality was also the best thing about him.

"But Mom," I said, "why don't you go and stay with one of your friends, if that's what you want? Look, I moved out because I wanted to be on my own. You know, thinking I couldn't depend on you forever."

"No one else knows about Dad, do they? You're the only one in the world. Well, maybe except for that woman who died with him, but I doubt we could ever be friends, and she's dead, besides. And with a friend I'd have other things to worry about. The only one I can really count on lives in San Francisco, where her husband's been posted," Mom said. "I guess I could go stay with her—they have a big guest suite—but I wouldn't like to impose that much. Maybe in a while, when we've gotten sick of living with each other, I could go visit for a month or so, but I could stay over there for years and it would still only be an escape from everything, you know?

"Here though—if I stay in Japan, whatever I do, it'll lead to the start of my new life, even if I don't quite know how. And I ought to save some money, since we don't know what the future will bring. I can pay the rent on this place no problem, and if you're my roommate I can feel free to leave any time. I don't know, there's no point worrying too much, is there? It's just the two of us, and there isn't enough money for luxuries. But I don't want to have to decide everything now—it seems trivial, and like admitting that I've lost. Let's worry about tomorrow when it comes."

I was impressed that Mom had turned into someone who could feel this way.

While Dad had only had a faint grasp on life, Mom had always been the responsible one. Everything was always planned for, no action wasted.

Mom was an only child, and her parents had passed away when I was young. Her childhood home, with its extensive orchards and pastures, had been sold off years ago. It was out in the middle of nowhere in Hokkaido, so it couldn't have sold for that much, but my stay-at-home mom had inherited the money and put it all into savings. Financially speaking, it wasn't that irresponsible of Mom to live with me for a while. It might even enable me to put some money away, too.

The real issue, though, was that I wasn't yet fully fledged from the nest.

I needed somewhere of my own to come home to, and I wanted Mom to stay at the condo to give me that.

It was within such childish bounds that I'd gotten excited about having the freedom to be on my own as much as I liked, and that was all I was really prepared for. I'd dreamed of life on my own on my own terms.

So having to share my own space, filled with only a few of my own things, felt like coming back down to earth with a bump. Especially when I'd even vowed not to live together with a lover if I found one, but to visit each other's places, while I was still in training, at least.

To properly honor my own independence, I probably should have made her leave—gotten angry, shouted, whatever it took. I'm sure that's what I would have done if I'd been her son.

But just then, Mom was looking out at Chazawa-Dori in the drizzle with her elbows on the windowsill and her chin in her hands, like a young girl.

To me, it was the most moving sight in the world.

The arguments that had been going round and round in my head suddenly fell quiet.

I understood, from seeing her there, that all she wanted

was to stay here for a while. There was a dreamlike vagueness to Mom's shape, in place of the definite outline of a grown woman. An unstable, indeterminate quality belonging to a young person, made of possibility and hope and loneliness.

"When you say that making plans would mean admitting you've lost," I said, "What do you mean—lost to what? Dad?"

"Not Dad," she said, "I'm talking about the lie that says you have to live a proper life, or else you'll be ruined. I worked so hard to be respectable, because I was afraid of what would happen. But what's happened has been, well, far worse than I could have expected.

"I can't believe the thing I'm most thankful for right now is that he died before getting into debt. Even though there's almost nothing left for us after he spent most of his savings on her. But he was always kind—he would have thought it was better to die than to put us in difficult straits. A kind of misplaced innocence, don't you think?

"A long time ago, before you were born, we went through a rough patch. He said he wasn't cut out for being a family man, and asked me if I'd divorce him, and maybe I should have agreed. But we talked about it, and decided to have you, and he never brought it up again. Once you were born he only said how wonderful marriage was, after all—he said that a lot.

"I'm not saying it was my fault that he died. I just want to rebel completely against everything in society that beat it into me that life would turn out okay if I only did the right things," said Mom.

I could hardly argue with that. I said to myself, *Okay, that was then, and this is now. Why don't I try changing my perspective: I'm on vacation, and Mom's just visiting. No big deal.*

I felt lighter almost immediately.

I knew I didn't want to reject her, so I simply accepted that there was no other option for now. We'd probably end up getting tired of each other at some point. I could work out what to do next when we got there.

The tension that left my body just then was probably the power of my habit of Planning Too Far Ahead. Right now, Mom was here, wanting to stay. That was the only sure thing—in a couple of days, she might change her mind and want to go home after all. But here I was, getting worked up about sticking to my plan, and getting all bent out of shape trying to do it.

"Sure, no problem," I said. "It's fine. I get it."

"Good, thanks," said Mom, matter-of-factly.

She probably knew me enough to know I couldn't refuse, and had thought of the conversation as a formality, and a waste of time. I felt a little vexed at being so predictable, but let it go. It was my own fault for not having the strength to say no.

I went to the window and sat down next to her.

What must it be like for your life to suddenly be a blank page, at her age? I wondered. No young children who needed her energy, no need to scramble to make ends meet. Only the dark, heavy shadow of regret that clung constantly to us both.

In some ways, whether we lived together here or not, we could never get back to where we'd been before, whatever we did. I knew we'd have to carry this for the rest of our lives. Even when there were brighter times that made it seem like we'd been able to forget for a moment, at the bottom of it there was always that shadow. We already knew from painful experience that life was about walking forward carrying the weight of it all. Even when we cried and raged until our throats were ragged and bleeding, there was no relief. We just carried on, pretending it didn't hurt.

At the condo, whose very layout defined the kind of average, respectable family who lived there, our roles too clear-cut, it was difficult to speak freely.

"Yocchan, do you think we were too square?" Mom asked.

"I don't think so," I said, "compared to most families. Maybe because there was a musician in the house, but I think we were pretty free."

Dad kept late hours, and there was music playing all the time at the house. When he had friends visiting they'd party all night, or jam quietly, and I even got time off school so Mom and I could tag along to "help" when Dad toured abroad: Thailand, Shanghai, Boston and New York, Paris, Korea, and Taiwan. It wasn't luxury travel, but there was always music. Sometimes there were other kids on the tour bus I made friends with, or had small crushes on, and it was a carefree, hippyish childhood.

"Then maybe it was me that was square," Mom said.

"Well, of course, a little, but someone had to be," I said. "The household wouldn't have functioned otherwise. Besides," I said, psyching myself up to admit something I'd been thinking since I was a child, "if it hadn't been for us, I think Dad would have been dead a long time ago."

Mom looked at me with her eyes wide. She didn't say it, but I clearly saw a kind of confirmation there, which said, *You thought so, too?*

"Thanks," she said instead.

Chazawa-Dori didn't get a lot of traffic, and the cars that did pass went by with an easy flow, like people walking along.

Opposite the window was Les Liens, the bistro where I worked. Weak lamplight glowed through the old windowpanes of Mikenekosha, the coffee shop above it. In the misty rain, everything looked like it was dissolving wanly into the evening.

Was Mom going to turn into a lunchtime regular at my workplace? *I didn't predict any of this*, I thought ruefully. *I won't change a thing. Let me not go out and get her guest towels, or extra cups—she can have the whole staying-with-friends experience. I'll let her sleep on the spare futon mattress, like any visitor.* Right now, the tired bedding here—although I had sprung for feather in the comforters—would provide more comfort to Mom than the expensive Tempur mattresses back at home.

When I got home later tonight, all wrung out, I'd surely be aggrieved to find her here. That was normal—that was how it should be. I gave myself permission to feel as exasperated as I liked.

"Plus," Mom said suddenly, almost as an afterthought, "I can't stay at home because of Dad's ghost."

"You're joking," I said.

"I swear. If I wake up while it's still dark he'll be sleeping on the other side of the bed as usual, or I'll look over and see him sitting on the sofa," she said.

"Mom, have you lost your mind to grief?" I said. "You never used to believe in things like that. When I scared myself watching kids' horror shows on TV, you'd tell me they were absurd, and brush me off."

"Which is precisely why you should believe me when I say so. I don't believe it either, but I was starting to feel like I was going crazy, which is why I came here. As if anyone would tumble into their daughter's cheap lodgings unless they had to," she said, calmly. "Shall we have a cup of tea, or something? Can you brew us a pot?"

"What kind would you like?" I said.

"Black tea. Sitting by this window drinking tea makes me feel like I'm in a café. Can we buy a little café table? You know that place that refurbishes antique furniture, over there? I came across it yesterday, when I was taking a walk down Inokashira-Dori, and I've fallen head over heels. I stayed and watched them work—all those young men in short sleeves with their muscular arms, grappling with the furniture, sanding and varnishing and making good . . . it's really something. It makes me want to tap that," she said.

"That place, yeah, it's great, isn't it. And cheap. I agree, this place suits older stuff better, and I don't mind if you're buying it. We could use it as a dinner table, too. Plus you could stalk me from the window while I'm at work . . . anyway, I'll put the kettle on," I said, getting up. Inside I was wondering where on earth she'd picked up a phrase like *tap that*. In this neighborhood full of young people, Mom was probably trying to acclimatize to the language, like a person who'd just arrived in a foreign country.

"Hey Mom, where did you put that new season Darjeeling you brought from home?"

"Oh, in the refrigerator."

"Cool."

We could have had this exact conversation back at home, I thought, opening the fridge door. *So much for me flying the nest!*

But never mind, I told myself. *Here is not there, and now is not then.* This was the only today we had.

This could be the last time I get to live with Mom, I thought. *For all I know . . .* my stomach clenched. She might be more desperate than she appeared, and could disappear just like Dad had. Then, in an instant, I'd never be able to be near her again.

If the alternative was for her to die back at the condo, tormented by the idea that she was seeing things, or even—not that I believed this, but hypothetically, if it was real—to keep living alongside Dad's ghost, I'd unquestionably prefer her to be here, even if she was putting a damper on my new life.

Hugging her knees and leaning on the cushions by the window, Mom seemed delicate and insubstantial.

This was a new town for me, too. Being here with her, almost having fun, I felt like I was getting to start over.

I put our tea on a tray and took it over to the window, and sat with her.

"So," I said.

"What?" Mom said, surprised.

"Tell me about Dad's ghost. I want to know," I said.

"I told you everything already," she said. "Sometimes, at home, he's just *there*. And I get confused. He doesn't speak, or make eye contact or anything; just wanders around, like he used to do. We share the space, like we're the air we breathe, and it feels so familiar. It feels so normal, I lose track of what's real and what's not."

She sounded so matter-of-fact that I nearly got fooled into thinking, *Right, okay.*

"But wait," I said, "what if he's still wandering around the condo on his own, now that you're not there? Is it safe to leave him there? Won't it . . . stop his soul from departing this earth and getting to the afterlife, or something? Don't you feel sorry for him?"

Mom looked down and gave a little huff, like she was trying to suppress a laugh. "You mean he'll kill himself otherwise? Or someone else will?"

True, I thought. The worst that could happen had already happened.

Mom said, "Yocchan, why should we have to worry about whether Dad's lonely, after he went and committed suicide with another woman? I mean, that must be the worst way to die, if you're talking about reaching the afterlife. It's not like we'd be the ones stopping him."

"You're right," I said. "But we could get the place cleansed, so he can start the journey, or something?"

"I'm not ruling it out," said Mom, "but right now I'm still kind of furious. I'm not an expert, but isn't there no point doing stuff like that until you've truly forgiven them, from the bottom of your heart?"

I wasn't angry at Dad, because he was my parent. All I felt was pity at how he'd gone so far down that lonesome road, which had been as dark as the night just before dawn.

No matter how warm a family we'd been, between me not being home much anymore, and Mom not being as in love with Dad as she once was, we could hardly have been enough of a draw to call him back home. Young children kept a family together like glue, but I'd grown up. We hadn't been able to compete with that woman's bewitching allure.

In spite of all that, I missed him. We hadn't even seen each other much, toward the end, but when we did, I always knew that he loved me completely.

Obviously, though, it wasn't so simple for Mom, since they'd been a couple. She and I were both family, but our positions were irreconcilably different. Even while he was alive, Dad had been like a hologram projected between us, showing us each a different image. Now that he was dead—or a ghost, according to Mom—this was clearer than ever.

We'd only ever gone anywhere as a family while I was young. Once I was grown, I might do stuff with each of them separately, but we were only together as a family at his gigs. And after Mom and I found out about several women that he'd had affairs with—nothing serious, and probably just emotional— Mom lost her taste for witnessing his personal relationships up close, and used to leave and take me out to eat somewhere rather than stay for the after-party.

If Dad had been a drinker, would he have died even earlier? Or would it have made it easier for him to keep his life in balance? I always wondered, and I'd never know. Although he couldn't hold his liquor, Dad—always prone to feeling lonely— enjoyed going out drinking with people, and often came home from parties after dawn. To other people he might have only been a skinny keyboard player, just another interchangeable musician out of so many, but to me, he was my only Dad.

Dad's band was a fairly standard five-piece, but they often invited guest musicians from different genres and backgrounds to play with them to mix things up. Marimba players, mbira players, quena players, jazz musicians—even dancers. The more people were involved in a gig, the less money they each got paid—but Dad's love for music was so steadfast, it didn't pain him to have to take on more work because of that. Sometimes people called his playing boring, because of just how seriously he took the music, and how it always came first with him. That was another thing I loved about him.

Even as a teenager, when I overheard the late night conversations between Dad, who'd come home after playing his heart out, and Mom, who'd kind of been waiting up for him, I felt safe, like I was a young child again.

When Dad came through the door, Mom would come out of the bedroom, and they'd talk mellowly about how the gig had gone, who'd turned up, or where she'd taken me for food afterward. Dad would address everything patiently, sounding relieved. The most important thing for him, at the end of a long day, was catching up with Mom over the little things. I know this because he told me so himself. "It's the best thing about being married," he used to say, so often it sounded like habit. "People you can share the little things with are few and far between."

I wondered if Dad had felt lonely when he got killed, without Mom there to talk to. Whether his spirit was hanging around, feeling like there were things he'd left unsaid. There had to be—he wouldn't have known he was going to die that day. Well, I guessed most people didn't, but I was sure he didn't expect to be killed by the person he was with. Was he scared? Or did he think, deep down, that it would somehow turn out okay?

Even though I didn't believe in ghosts, I could hardly bear to think about this.

I wasn't sure—being still too much of a child not to wish that things could be definitely one thing or another—but I suspected that people couldn't always be true to themselves, or live wholly for the proper and acceptable things in their lives. But perhaps they held themselves together by acting as though they were happy with their own choices, because they'd fall apart if they didn't at least aim to be, and it was too uncomfortable to admit that they weren't.

For Dad, his music, having fun with me, the almost dead-end stability of his relationship with Mom, or the fact that her indistinct expectations hung like a mist and put pressure on him like he was packed in cotton wool—each of these things might have contributed a little to the way he'd died. Mom was a very strong personality, and it could sometimes feel a little stifling just to be around her.

What made me sad was that Dad was the only one who knew how he'd really felt. That I could never know the truth—and that Dad himself probably hadn't been able to stand to look at it any longer.

My days at the bistro were so busy they made my head spin.

I opened up the kitchen first thing in the morning. I'd mix and knead the bread dough and leave it to rise, then put the chairs up in the dining room and start cleaning. At the same time, I put water on to boil, and prepped the vegetables for sides and salads. I checked stock levels, and topped things up if we were running low. Then I'd bake off three or four dozen loaves.

Then Michiyo-san, the chef, would turn up and I'd assist her with whatever she needed help with, until customers turned up and I'd switch to serving. From there, time passed in a whirlwind until two thirty.

Our staff meal at three thirty was always incredibly delicious, and sometimes I'd ask Michiyo-san to show me how it was made. Then I had my break, and on days when I had no other plans, I'd take a walk around the neighborhood, or go home and take a nap. At dinner service, most customers would linger over drinks, and we'd be at closing time before I knew it.

At weekends, which tended to be hectic, I had help in the form of Moriyama-san, a friendly man who was an expert on wine. But even during the week, when it was only me, I had hardly any downtime. We usually had a full house, and didn't turn a lot of tables, since our customers tended to take their time. That was the kind of restaurant it was. That said, we also had customers who came in for a quick beer or a glass of wine during the day, so we always had to have some simple hors d'oeuvres on the menu, in addition to the lunch dishes.

I was in charge of the hors d'oeuvres and the appetizers, so I'd take any spare moment I had to wash vegetables or do other prep. It was also my job to clean the dining room and keep the glassware polished.

The bistro wasn't in Ginza, where the best French restaurants were, or in a upscale neighborhood like Aoyama or Azabu. It wasn't even in the fashionable areas of Jiyugaoka or Hiro'o. But I had a personal reason for having set my heart on working at this particular bistro in Shimokitazawa.

FOR OBVIOUS REASONS, MOM completely lost her appetite after Dad died. She stayed in bed a lot, and when she was up and not talking to me, she was always talking to herself, whispering, "It's not true, it can't be true."

She refused to set up the usual altar in the house, saying she just couldn't believe he was gone. She did put up a photo in the room that contained Dad's piano and his beloved speakers and valve amplifier, and kept fresh flowers there, so it wasn't that she didn't understand what was real. She just couldn't accept it.

"I feel like he's going to come back through the door any day now," she'd say.

For some reason, my reality had kept up to date with everything that had happened—his body, the business of organizing the funeral and putting his ashes in the tomb, even seeing the photo of that woman who'd died at the same time. So I didn't have the same sense of disbelief as Mom did.

Even so, I constantly wondered—*Why had it come to this? Why hadn't he talked to us? Had I been too distant from him? Had there ever been a time when he might have wanted to talk, and I'd passed him in the hallway and gone to bed oblivious?* Around and around, I'd remember, wonder, regret, wonder again, forget for a moment, and then plunge back into the cycle.

ON HIS LAST MORNING, I saw Dad in the entry of the condo, about to leave.

"Hey, when you're done with these gigs, maybe next week, will you take me out for some expensive French food in Aoyama?" I'd said.

"How expensive are we talking about, here?" Dad said, putting on his shoes.

"Umm, around the fifteen thousand yen mark. Not including drinks. Somewhere with a really good wine list," I said.

"You're not kidding, that's pretty expensive!" he said, and laughed, with his tattered Boston bag at his feet like a loyal dog.

He'd told us he was going out to a friend's venue in Ginza to fill in at a gig that evening. That much, at least, was true. After making a brief appearance at the after-party, Dad left Tokyo in the woman's car, took a room at an inn at a hot spring bath in Ibaraki, where he told the manager he was going out to eat, had dinner at a local *izakaya*, and then died.

When Dad didn't come home that night, Mom and I hadn't thought it was a big deal, even though he'd basically never done that before.

He forgot his phone, I'd said. *Do you think he left it on purpose so we couldn't reach him, knowing he'd be getting into trouble?*

I hate him, Mom had said. *I won't let him in the door when he comes back.*

I'd handed him his bag as he left the house, and he'd put it on his shoulder.

"I need to eat lots of good food so I can educate my palate," I said.

"That's true. Let's make a date when I get back," Dad said. He looked a little sad.

That *when I get back* hadn't been a lie. He'd had no intention of dying that day.

"I wish I could come with you and see the gig, but I promised a friend to help out at their café in the evening. Someone got sick, and they're shorthanded," I said.

"You could still join us in Ginza afterward. I won't have a lot of stage time, though; I'm only guesting," he said.

"No, it'll be too late by the time I'm finished. Save our date for Aoyama," I said, and laughed.

"Sure thing. I'll see you later," he said, and floated out the door. I saw a flutter of his familiar blue short-sleeved shirt out of the corner of my eye. That was the last time he walked out that door alive.

Over and over, I rewind the scene, replay it. *Okay, I'll see you there, Dad.* No—it's not enough. *Let me come with you right now, I don't need to bring anything.* Over and over I regret not saying that. I could have clung to his legs, wept and asked him not to go, made it impossible for him to leave. Fallen to the floor and pretended to faint and made him stay.

I kept noticing myself trying to redo the scene in my head, even though I knew it was impossible. The more I replayed it, the clearer the fake images got, while Dad's real memory faded.

FOR A LONG TIME after Dad died, neither Mom nor I could muster up much of an appetite.

One Sunday afternoon, Mom and I were in the apartment, feeling trapped and stifled. We should have been hungry, but eating was the last thing we wanted to do.

I thought about fixing some food. Even soup or congee seemed too heavy. I'd bought some vegetables for a salad, but their freshness and greenness felt so blinding, I didn't think I could eat them.

"Hey, Mom? Can you think of anything you feel like eating? Let's get something in our bellies. Or we'll feel even more miserable," I said. I was stroking Mom's warmish back as she lay in bed, crying messily.

Out of nowhere, she said, "I could go for a shave ice."

It was a sweltering summer. The kind where you felt if you took one step outside you'd be steamed alive by the heat rising from the asphalt, and the heat hung around even at night and stopped you from breathing.

No wonder they kept Dad's body on ice, given how hot it's been. The thought came to me suddenly, quietly.

The deep blue of the sky outside the window matched the way I felt. *I can't believe you're not here anymore, Dad.*

I forced Mom to get up, and we pulled on some clothes over our pajamas, got into a taxi, and headed to Shimokitazawa. I was thinking of a place I'd been a few times with friends that had the best shave ice I'd ever eaten: Les Liens.

When we entered the restaurant, our bodies were immediately drawn into the cozily muddled atmosphere, a combination of hot air rushing in from outside and chill wafting from the air-conditioning. We gravitated toward the small table at the back by a window, sat down, and sighed.

The high summer sun coming through the glass was steadily burning my right arm. Mom was staring out at something outside. No matter where we went, we were a sorry sight— miserable, pathetic, and abandoned.

The pretty chef with the good posture—whom I now call Michiyo-san, but whose name I didn't know at the time—smiled and told us we had plenty of time, so we ordered two shave ices with mango, white peach, and blackcurrant.

The ice was delicate, and the fruit was truly ambrosial. The sweetness slipped into our hearts and our stomachs, like food from heaven. I could feel my mind, overheated from endless cycles of questioning and doubt and regret, relax into cool repose.

Even the occasional waves of hot air entering through the front door felt comforting.

"I feel like I might be getting hungry," Mom said.

The restaurant was in a renovated old building, with an interior reminiscent of a bistro in a Paris backstreet, and that sensation of being outside the everyday put us at ease. After surviving on what little we could keep down—mugs of café au lait, cookies, sachets of powdered soup—we found our appetites for the first time in a long time, and ordered a big barley salad to share. It arrived topped with crispy toasted French bread, and plenty of barley and *jambon cru*, with baby corn and cherry tomatoes and cucumber and okra mixed into a bed of lettuce.

"Wow, I can taste this—it tastes good. I'd almost forgotten what it feels like to taste. I guess the body lives, even if your heart's died," said Mom, in a small, hollow voice.

We wolfed down the salad, like we had the shave ices, and drank coffee, and finally settled. It felt like the first time in months.

We stared out the window. The time passing in the bistro felt natural, like it was all our own, safe from intrusion.

We'd forgotten time could even feel that way.

We'd been carrying around a sense of someone missing—someone we might be able to find if only we knew where to go, then things might become clear.

We didn't cry then and there in the bistro, but the feeling of the cells in our bodies welcoming the sudden influx of nutrients was as refreshing as crying in a speeding car with the windows rolled down, letting tears fly. Like finally sitting yourself down at your destination at the end of an exhausting journey.

Michiyo-san didn't know what we were going through, nor did she console us directly. All she did was put herself into her food and offer it to us. That was obvious in everything about the restaurant—everything there was as real and as certain as anything could be.

For a while after that, Mom and I went there regularly, one or the other of us suggesting the outing whenever we started feeling discouraged or down. We shared salads, and reset with shave ices, and somehow got through the rock bottom that was that summer. We'd both lost weight and become a little unsteady, but whenever we went to the bistro, we managed to work through the menu like a happy mother and child.

For some reason, the summer afternoons, and evenings when the sky turned pink, and all the times I found myself there absorbed in looking out the windows or down at the floor, now live on in my mind like something wonderful and priceless.

Summer ended, as did shave-ice season, but we kept going to Les Liens all through that fall and winter.

By the time the cherry tree outside the Tsuyusaki Building, which housed the restaurant, was in full bloom, both Mom and I had recovered enough to be eating and drinking normally. Even so, when our appetites flagged, or staying in the apartment became unbearable, one of us would say, "I might be able to manage the barley salad," which would be the signal for us to get on the bus or a taxi and get to Les Liens.

THUS IT WAS ALMOST inevitable that when I moved out to live on my own, I got a job at Les Liens, and built my new life around my work there by renting an apartment across the street.

The pay wasn't great, and I knew it would be hard work given that Shimokitazawa was something of a tourist destination.

But I couldn't have asked for a better distraction. Yes—the most important thing for me at that point was to find some relief from the thoughts in my head.

The excitement of not knowing who would come through the door; the thrill of using both my body and my mind at once; the awareness that the restaurant was something like an amoeba, a living thing that responded to my every move—it all suited me down to the ground. I was also starting to see the value that training here would have for my future career.

Les Liens never let it be an option for me to leave the water in the vases unchanged because I felt a little slow that day, or to go ahead and bake the *choux* pastry dough even though the texture was slightly off.

I was starting to understand that not stopping to fix little internal niggles like these always came back to you, and sooner than you might expect. This was probably even more true when it came to food, which as humans we tended to respond to on an instinctual level. Even if you kept something a secret at first, held it close to your chest, it always came out in some form or another. The only thing to do was to work steadily, humbly, and carefully, without trying to complicate things or make them other than what they were.

I sometimes thought that if Dad had been more of an epicure, he'd have had another thing to enjoy—something that might have been able to keep him anchored in this world.

Dad was never that excited by eating, but he always made an effort with anything I made. Mom even got a little jealous sometimes because he always cleared his plate. "Someday," he'd said once, "when you've opened your own restaurant, I'll come and have a full-course meal. Do my best with the wine. I'll have to stay alive until then," he'd said. And yet . . .

I felt a little cheated. A few years ago, I'd been nowhere near as good a cook as I was now. But my cooking then was all Dad was ever going to know of my food. For Dad, my cooking would be stuck at that stage forever.

On the other hand, it also inspired a more constructive desire to cook things that even people who didn't eat that well, like Dad, would enjoy. To create a space that could nourish and empower people just by their being in it, and make them think maybe eating wasn't so bad after all.

That was something Dad had said, a few years ago, when I'd made him a small rice omelette.

"I never really understood the fuss until now—I thought food just needed to be edible. But when your own daughter makes you something like this, it's really something special. Maybe this eating thing's not so bad after all."

My life in Shimokitazawa revolved entirely around the bistro.

If I woke up and Mom was still asleep, I'd get worried she was going to stay in bed all day, but thankfully that never happened. Once I got up and got going, Mom would get up too and make me coffee, even though she didn't have to.

When I first discovered the coffee that Mom made when she didn't have to, I was shocked at how strong, hot, fragrant, and delicious it was.

Up until now, all the things Mom had done to take care of me she'd done out of habit or obligation. Now, she made us coffee so we could enjoy it together. The difference it made was astonishing.

Mom never fixed me breakfast, either. That was good, too.

The most she did was shape rice balls from last night's rice, or put sweet pastries out on a plate. Other days I'd pull out a chilled ratatouille I put together from vegetables leftover from the bistro. We'd pick at these and watch morning TV, and chat a little. Things that had nothing to do with us being mother and daughter, like *Do you think this is a little too salty for breakfast?—I agree, it might go better with wine.* Even so, living with Mom, I felt more at ease than I would have done otherwise. I could stay out late with no qualms, and surprisingly, my impatience never got the better of me. Living together worked well on the basis that I was almost never home, but the apartment was very clearly my space.

Mom cleaned pretty regularly, but not perfectly like she used to. The condo in Meguro had always been spotless, because Dad liked things tidy and went around putting things in order whenever he had a spare moment.

Mom didn't peek at my cell phone or messages out of curiosity anymore, either. She played around on her own phone, and didn't pry into my life. If I went to meet old friends over drinks on a day off and came home late, she didn't seem especially interested or ask many questions. I finally realized that all the times she'd been strict about my curfew or had seemed much more interested in my life back when I was a student, she'd simply been carrying out a role.

In the mornings when I was running late and rushing to get dressed, Mom would send a cheery *Have a good day!* over my way. She said it differently from the way she used to say it as my mother. I couldn't have said how, exactly. But it sounded more free, like she was thinking only of her own day as it lay ahead.

Another thing that felt new to me was how Mom, with her slightly tubby figure, took to dressing in a small selection of T-shirts and sweatshirts with jeans, her belly perched on the waistband of her jeans. At home, she wore a matching set of thick men's sweatshirts and sweatpants that she'd bought at a boutique catering to young people, halfway down the main street. Some days it seemed like she lay about at home all day, while on others she seemed to go out eagerly, although I had no idea what she got up to during the day.

This was our new normal for a while.

Aside from her new wardrobe of youthful clothing, and a vintage Fire-King mug with a picture of Snoopy from Peanuts that she'd bought in the neighborhood, she didn't even seem to be shopping much.

I'd expected her to struggle with all that free time, and be constantly coming in Les Liens, so I was a little taken aback.

I was seeing Mom outside of her role as mother for the first time.

For instance, she only bought one of the Snoopy mugs, for herself. That would never have happened before. She would have purchased a set of three, one for each of us, or a pair at the very least.

Was this what she was like when she was younger? I wondered. In college, falling in love, working part-time, had she lived frugally in a friend's cheap apartment, and sat by the window looking up at the sky?

She'd placed the small antique table she'd bought at Yamada Shoten next to the low stools which had been in the apartment when I moved in, but instead of sitting on a stool, she was sitting on the floor with her elbows on the seat, perched by the window like a puppy.

"Mom, what do you even do all day?" I asked.

"Not telling," she said, with a smile.

"Not fair! You know exactly where I go," I said.

"There," she said, and pointed out the window at the bistro with its old wooden door and triangular window.

"See?" I said. "I'm curious. I feel like the parent now, like we've switched roles."

It might have been my imagination, but Mom seemed to have lost a little weight, and her skin looked younger, after having been dry and pallid for so long. Today she was wearing a pale pink I [HEART] SHIMOKITA! T-shirt designed by Keiichi Sokabe, a cool rock musician who lived locally and owned a record store and café a few streets away. The T-shirt was pretty tight on her, so I almost said, *Mom, that color's not the most slimming*—but I restrained myself.

To go with it, she had on her usual vintage jeans, and bare feet, although it was getting cold. I couldn't believe it—Mom, who used to wear pantyhose even at the height of summer.

"There are a few different ways my day can go," she said. "But basically, I get up, and we have some breakfast, and take our time over good coffee, right? And I see you off, and watch you go through that door into the bistro. I can hear you say *Good morning!* as you go inside."

"I can't believe it," I said. "It's like parents' day at school."

"You can't go wrong while you can still greet people confidently. This is a fact. So it always reassures me. I think, *What a good girl Yocchan is, thank you god*," she said.

I didn't know what to say.

"After that I space out for a little, then clear things away. Wash the dishes, since you don't have a dishwasher. I put them in that basket, and, guess what, I leave them there. Drip-dry."

"Fair enough, we don't have that many dishes."

"Next, I do a light clean, with a duster and a broom and a dustpan and a rag. Easy peasy. I clean the toilet as well. I wish it wasn't Japanese-style, since I have to bend down more, but as a freeloader I can't complain."

"True," I said.

"Then I go on my cell phone and check my e-mail, and let people who want to see me know I've moved in with my daughter. If there's a package for me at the old place, well, I've asked the super to take care of it, but I still go back once in a while. Sometimes people send perishables and things. I don't see Dad's ghost anymore. I think it's because I'm feeling happier. More like—living there feeling all shadowy, I might have ended up slipping into his world, maybe."

"Let's go back together sometime," I said. "I miss Dad too, ghost or not."

"Okay, let's go back together when we have to, the next time someone sends us food, or there's a residents' meeting. I still don't feel like staying there overnight, but you can take a boyfriend there if you want to. Just tell me where you are so I don't worry. Well, I will anyway, a little, but I'm sure things will go fine once they taste your cooking. Feel free to open a good bottle of wine—I've left the wine cooler on. I brought one back the other week and drank the whole thing. I'm sorry, I didn't even tell you," she said.

"I spotted the empty when I took the trash out," I said. "But you know, I'm too busy to be staying the night with anyone right now."

"When I worked in a jazz café, back in the day, customers were always dropping in to see me, all day long. I went on a lot of dates," Mom said, seeming disappointed. "Anyway, then at lunchtime I take my purse and my keys and my cell phone, and wander out.

"First, I stop by One Love on Pure Road, just over there, and browse the old books—I can never quite tell what's for sale, and what's the owner Hacchan's personal collection—and chat to Hacchan a little. Stuff like our hopes for the future, or how baffling the modern world can be, that kind of thing.

"And gardening. How to get lotus to bloom. He says he'll have some tubers to share at replanting time, early next year, so we'll be able to have lotus flowers here by the windowsill, too. There's a cool local gardener called Mr. Tanba who's an expert on lotus, and he'll come out and plant them up for you, with the right mix of fertilizer in the soil and everything. Doesn't that sound exciting? How refreshing would it be to have big lotus flowers right there by the window once summer comes around? Anyway, that's the kind of thing we gossip about, and Hacchan always makes some good strong English tea, and sometimes I tidy up around the place for him as a thank-you," she said.

"Since when are you so close with that old guy?" I asked, slightly reeling from the revelation that Mom planned to still be here next year.

"We're neighbors! And we're around the same age, you know, so I couldn't help getting to know him if I passed by.

"Anyway, after that, I either go to the traditional tea house and say hi to Eri-chan the manager and the pet tortoises, and order the Japanese tea of the day along with some rice crackers or sweet dumplings, and take my time over refills, or I go to the coffee shop and have cinnamon toast, with strong coffee and lots of whipped cream on the side. Or, if it's a day when the Thai restaurant's open for lunch, I have their papaya salad with sticky rice. That chef Miyuki's Thai food is something else! She grinds up the spices and things right there in front of you. I never really liked Thai food that much until I tasted hers. She and your chef, Michiyo, are definitely the standout cooks around here.

"So that's about how my afternoon usually goes. I love getting pizza at Rokusan, or La Verde's is good too. I can easily polish off a whole one on my own. Occasionally I splurge and get a traditional full-course lunch at Asuka. And the whole time, I'm slowly making my way through *In Search of Lost Time*, which I never got a chance to read. I got the books from Hacchan's—I rented the whole set for two thousand yen; well, actually, he said I could borrow them, even though his shop's a bookstore and not a lending library, so I kind of just left some money with him.

"Speaking of books, and I know this is pretty fannish of me, but whenever I hear the writer Osamu Fujitani's got a new book coming out, I go to the bookstore called Ficciones that he runs himself, upstairs near the hamburger place, buy the book and get it autographed, and then run to the café above your bistro and read it from cover to cover. Then I compose a letter with my thoughts on the book and slip it through the letterbox at Ficciones. How very decadent! Mr. Fujitani's not only a fantastic writer, he's also incredibly good-looking. He has a great voice, and tells such funny stories, is so sophisticated and—most importantly—whip-smart, plus he has lovely big hands. He's just as intellectual and funny as the main characters in his books. I'm a huge fan. He just gives me such a thrill! He's the kind of man I wish I could have married, to tell the truth.

"Further inside the building where Mr. Fujitani's shop is, there's also a Thai massage salon, run by a studious young man called Hirota-san. I saw an ad and decided to take a chance, but what do you know, getting stretched by a young person really makes you feel rejuvenated. I don't indulge that often, but I sometimes go when I've got a headache, because that can clear it up instantly. I know you've been saying you get back pain. I bet Thai massage would really help. I'll bring you there any time.

"What else? Sometimes I go to Taimado, the hemporium, and buy an outrageous T-shirt, or some lotion, or something. The people there are all really nice, even though they look quite outlandish. Then I'll go to their restaurant, and have some hemp food. It really clears you out, that stuff.

"The day passes pretty quickly when I go for one of these options. And it costs hardly anything.

"Otherwise, I walk down to Sangenjaya to the big Tsutaya to browse magazines, or get bread from the famous sourdough bakery. You know the soft raisin loaf we sometimes have for breakfast? After that I go to the cute café round the back of the Carrot Tower, and have a cup of coffee and a bean-based dessert. I like acting as if I'm on vacation like that. It helps me feel like I've achieved something.

"The main thing I'm careful of is to really take my time when I'm walking. Go slowly, like I used to when I was a student. Because that's all I've got now. Time."

"It sounds fun. Like a life of leisure," I said, impressed.

"You know how the flow of time through a day slows down around late afternoon, and then quickens again after the sun goes down? I finally recovered my ability to sense it, recently, and now I can get in touch with that flow each day.

"I can sense the border between when time dribbles on and stretches, like a warm rice cake, and when it suddenly pulls in tight, and speeds up again. I love being able to do that. I look forward to it every day.

"I'd forgotten about it, you know? Even though when I was a kid, I sensed it no problem, even if I stayed inside all day.

"That's the kind of phase I'm in right now. I want to let myself take in the flow of time again, without having to think or worry about anything.

"I feel like if I was back at the apartment, I might spend my days like Dad was still there. As though I was married to a ghost. Lining up shoes in the entry, cleaning, making something to eat, putting the leftovers in the freezer, throwing them out after a month. Feeling like a robot.

"I know there are shops and restaurants I could go to, back in Meguro, and people I could see. But those are people who met me when I was married with one daughter to a musician who played keyboards for singers who were well respected, if not famous. In Shimokitazawa I'm no one, just a washed-up middle-aged woman. And that's okay, here.

"That said, it's not like I always feel fine. There are times I want to rip my hair out, wondering what I'm playing at. Plenty of days when nothing feels right, and I'm frustrated, and my feet feel like lead, or when I don't see the point in anything and I spend the whole day here in bed. But on better days, I can feel it—time stretching and shrinking. Anyway, the fact I can talk about this means I'm doing pretty well. I was lucky enough to meet and marry the man I loved without ever having had my heart broken, and once we were together, I didn't have too much trouble with my mother-in-law or anything, so I've never felt low for this long without being able to get out before, except maybe when my parents died. But I wasn't living with them at that point, so even then it wasn't like my daily life was destroyed, like now. It's almost like my body had totally forgotten how to grieve.

"You know, I'm not a real resident, and it's not like I'd campaign against it, or anything, but I worry that if they built a big new building by the station, the people who ended up working there would keep disappearing and getting replaced with new people all the time, even if we said hello and got to know them just like we do with our neighbors now. They could get moved to a different branch of the chain store, or quit because they were only temping anyway. And the ingredients they'd use might get delivered frozen from some central factory, and you wouldn't get to hear those interesting and relatable stories about what was good at the market that morning, or how the new dish they were developing didn't turn out, that kind of thing? I'm just making all this up in my head, I know, but this is what I picture.

"It takes time to get to know people, let alone to tell whether you like each other, so it really makes me wonder, you know, what you're supposed to do if they just keep coming through like a revolving door, in one day and out another, and you don't even have time to figure out who they are?

"It seems like there are a lot of people in this town who've been here a long time. And those people are mostly around my age, give or take half a generation, which takes the pressure off. I don't have to pretend to be anything, so I can just step out the door as I am.

"Of course, I know this is all an illusion. It's not like I work hard to make a living and live in this neighborhood."

"It's not just an illusion, Mom," I said. "You've got your feet on the ground this whole time, even while you're also slightly floating above things. I feel like after you spent so long taking care of Dad, and raising me, managing the finances and running the house, being solidly in that role, it's okay for you to keep living like this for now. For me, too, even living with you as though we were just friends, I feel like you're giving me a lot of strength."

"How kind you are, Yocchan," Mom said. "I should be grateful for you listening to me whine for so long. When I was alone I thought my head would explode with all the regrets I have.

"Because—if I'd really done all those things as well as you say, how could he have left us like he did?" Mom said.

"You're wrong," I said. "I'm saying it again and I'll say it as many times as it takes. Dad was a good person, and I loved him, and he provided for us, but what happened to him was in no way your fault. I don't know what he was really thinking, but never having drunk, or partied, or gambled, and on top of that never having wanted to be famous or anything like that,

I think the problem was that he took everything too seriously. And because of that, when he had an affair, he got in too deep, and ended up where he did," I said.

"None of his friends knew he was so seriously involved with anyone," Mom said. "At first I thought they were all trying to cover for him, or spare my feelings, but it seems they're all telling the truth. *Never seen her*, they said, *not at a gig, not at an after-party.* So who on earth was she? They might have gone back a long way, for all we know."

"I guess since she was a distant relation, they might always have known of each other," I said. "But maybe they reconnected recently, and went too far too fast? We packed away all his diaries and notebooks and letters without looking through them, so it's a possibility."

"I still can't believe he died without even giving us a call. Was it bad luck that he forgot his cell phone that day? Or did he leave it behind on purpose? I know there's no point wondering, but I can't help it.

"He was always a little clumsy, or maybe unlucky, when it came down to the important things. Even so, I think—even if he *was* having a love affair, even then—how could he die, just like that? Did we really mean so little to him?"

I nodded.

"When I start thinking like that, I know living like this is what I need to be doing," Mom said. "But I'm not trying to punish myself. It's like physical therapy. Plus, I've got you. If you weren't here, or if you'd refused to have anything to do with me after leaving home and starting out on your own, I might have got even more down. So thanks for having me."

I would have refused, if I hadn't been afraid you'd kill yourself, I thought but didn't say. In Mom's eyes I was probably still a child—a child who accepted and loved and wanted to spend time with her mother no matter what. Even if she might claim not to think of me that way anymore, she'd probably never truly accept it, deep down. I was scared, too, to look beneath the surface of my new independence and find out just how deep and wide the seams in the rock that connected me to her went. For now, it was best to live in a way that let me avoid having to confront it.

"Mom, what are you going to do with the condo?" I asked.

"I can't even begin to think about that right now," Mom said.

Her long eyelashes, which in Meguro she'd always kept groomed by going to the salon, were now unkempt and devoid of mascara. But the shape of her face somehow looked clearer and younger now than it had before.

"I don't think I'll be here forever, of course. But I can't see myself going back and living there, either," she said.

"If only you could ask Dad," I said. I meant it. If only we could get Dad's blessing, we could sell the condo and think about things afresh. Because of the nasty aftertaste of the way he'd died, the place had become a kind of stifling mausoleum.

"You're right," Mom said. "Then I could feel more confident about things. But maybe it's important to have this kind of period where we're in limbo, too."

That was a very adult way of looking at things, I thought.

"Fundamentally, all of the Meguro Madame lifestyle—the shopping, the lunches, the facials—is only trying to make up for an unfulfilled sex drive, or acting as an outlet for it," she said.

"Mom, I can't believe you're saying this. It sounds too true it's scary."

"Because it *is* true," Mom said. "But maybe Dad wanted one last shot at the real thing, too. He'd certainly been on good behavior until then, considering what other musicians can be like. I sometimes think he'd have been more suited to working in local government, or something.

"So the Madame life is kind of empty. Sure you can treat yourself to five-course meals, but in the end you're just wasting your husband's money. In my case it wasn't Dad's money, but it was my parents', so same thing. You can collect good wine, but it's never-ending. Pointless. Have it once in a while, and it's wonderful. But otherwise, it's empty. Because you're trying to momentarily placate something which deep down is a spiritual hunger with irrelevant things. And when you get to my age you can't even live very near your real friends, so you see them less and less," she said.

"I was totally convinced you were loving that privileged lifestyle," I said. "And I assumed you and Dad had settled into a different kind of phase of your relationship."

As far as those things went, Mom had been picture perfect.

"I remember your skirts always used to be floaty, fresh from the cleaners, the perfect length, and you took your Hermès bag whenever you left the house. If there was a handbook for the Meguro Madame lifestyle that said *Late forties, moderately fashion-conscious and moderately wealthy, dresses to avoid embarrassing her husband. Eats out at least once a week, French or Italian, and often goes to previews of art exhibitions by friends and acquaintances,* well, that was exactly the kind of person you looked like from the outside," I said.

"I feel like that's going a little too far," Mom said, "but I guess that was what I was aiming for."

I suddenly wondered whether Mom had ever even owned a T-shirt before. She used to be tastefully made up even just to go to the local shops, rarely left the house with bare legs, and always had her hair freshly styled, tied back neatly, or lightly curled.

"I don't know how I got that way," Mom said. "I won't blame Meguro, or say it was the influence of the moms at your private girls' school. It was my own fault. I started out thinking I'd just have to look the part to get by, and before I knew it the poison had seeped in and changed me inside. Well, maybe calling it poison is going too far. More like I was so busy keeping up with daily life that I slacked off spiritually.

"I feel like people imprint on what they experience when they're young, and then gradually grow into it. I don't even know when I lost sight of it, it was so long ago. I meant to ask, doesn't the actor Naoto Takenaka often eat at your restaurant?" she said, suddenly.

"It's hardly mine, Mom, but he does. He's pretty quiet, very polite," I said, surprised by the direction she'd suddenly taken.

"I spotted him sitting at the bar the other day, and remembered. When I was a girl, I'm pretty sure I idolized his wife, Midori Kinouchi. She was the kind of woman I wanted to be when I grew up," she said seriously.

"But you're nothing like her," I said, taken aback. I hadn't had a clue. "You've really strayed from your vision. In more ways than one."

"I know. I thought she was the prettiest, most beautiful woman. I had all her records, and even had posters of her up on my wall. I wanted to give Mr. Takenaka a big hug and tell him all about it, but I didn't have the guts. Back when Midori got taken in by that good-looking musician Tsugutoshi, I saw it all on TV and just wanted to tell her, *You're making a mistake! Don't go with him! Even though I can see why you'd want to!*"

"Please don't do that, Mom," I said, genuinely worried. This new, liberated Mom was capable of anything.

"All those things that used to give me strength—I left them behind, one by one," she said.

"No offense, Mom, but isn't that a classic case of getting together with a guy and, maybe not losing yourself, but taking on too much of his expectations?" I said. "Being a Meguro Madame, the grown-up sex appeal, the proper etiquette—all that sounds exactly like Grandma on Dad's side."

"I guess I got manipulated by a mama's boy."

"Well, I think it was partly your fault for accepting it, too," I said. "But I feel like the real you was probably a cute, boho kind of woman.

"Dad was always surrounded by rock chicks, but he always loved the elegant, powerful type, like Grandma was. He wanted you to be like that, and tried to raise me like a princess, too. And when that coincided with a period when he was earning big money, I guess you got sucked into it without even noticing," I said, having quickly Googled *Midori Kinouchi* on my computer and found some old footage on YouTube. I felt a little flustered at her otherworldly cuteness. Mom was looking closely, too, at the teen idol who had apparently been her starting point.

"Where did I go wrong, when I could have turned out like

this? And what am I supposed to do about it now? Go confront Mr. Takenaka, demand to know how I got to be so different from his wife?" Mom said.

"No idea, but I'm pretty sure that's not the solution," I said.

"I know that! Don't get all flustered—like you thought I actually might!" said Mom, finally cracking a smile.

"I don't mind what you do, but please don't harass our customers. Mr. Takenaka's a quiet kind of guy, he'd never show his face there again."

"Your Chef Michiyo is a real gem, though," Mom said. "I'm sure she must find it trying, deep down, to have the mother of one of her employees come in as a customer. But she never shows it. Even better, she doesn't give me special treatment either, so sometimes I even forget you work there. Although that's mostly because I tend to go in on days when you're not working, and it's that young man Moriyama-san there instead."

"You're saying you go in to the restaurant where I work, on days I happen not to be there?" I asked, surprised, since Michiyo-san had never mentioned anything about it.

"That's right. I sit at the bar and ask for a pot of tea and the *fromage blanc*. It's the best. The crispy orange bits on top, do you make those?"

"Yeah. I put a batch in the oven whenever I've got time, during prep or before dinner service. But, wow. I had no idea."

"It's awkward to go in when you're there, you know," Mom said.

"I mean, as a customer, you're welcome to come in any time," I said. I'd gotten a lot better recently at letting things like this go when it came to Mom.

"We had some on our trip to Paris, with Dad, do you remember? *Fromage blanc*. Wasn't that a great period for us as a family? I'm so glad we had that. We did the tourist thing and walked to the Deux Magots. And there really were two Chinamen up on the wall! After that, Dad dragged us to HMV, and then we went up the Arc de Triomphe," she said, reminiscing.

"I remember. It was pretty tiring, climbing all those steps," I said.

"It was wonderful looking down from the top at the streets stretching into the distance in all directions. I felt like Napoleon."

"I have to say that sounds a little suspect, Mom, both historically and emotionally," I said, laughing.

"Do you think so? Does it matter, as long as it's just what I think? Anyway, after that we went to a shop that sold Middle Eastern sandwiches, and ate them right there in the shop, even though it had no seats. And Dad said he'd never enjoyed so much garlic in a single meal," she said.

"We had a lot of good times, didn't we, as a family," I said. Our memories of that trip were shimmering into being between us, along with the sensation of Paris's cloudy skies. The three of us had really been there—had left our footprints on that foreign soil.

"No mistake about it," Mom said. "If you want to look back at the bad parts, well, the end was the worst by far. Overall, it wasn't that bad. Something went wrong, and we got thrown off course, and that's how we've ended up here." She smiled.

These conversations had become like rituals to us, recited like prayers.

We'd pull out a memory, and spend time in it.

Like rolling a piece of candy around in our mouths, we'd reminisce—about what we'd seen on a particular day in Paris, how we'd walked around its streets, what we'd talked about in the evening, the hotel room we'd stayed in—and breathe the memory in deeply. Then we'd come back to reality, and feel a little breathless.

I couldn't help but wonder. How many more of these conversations would it take before we could move forward?

Mom and Dad might have had their differences, but they were supposed to grow old together, companionably. I was going to get married and keep working and also have children, and we'd all go visit Mom and Dad back in Meguro every once in a while. That had been the plan.

Was Dad still playing the piano in that big, empty room in the condo? Wasn't he there, fixing himself some instant noodles? Had he absentmindedly pulled on mismatched socks like he often did? My chest felt tight with worry. Funny, when he was already gone.

He wouldn't have come back to the apartment to haunt it, I thought, if he'd really loved that woman. But I knew that even mentioning her would make Mom's expression tense and harden, just when she was reminiscing fondly, so I didn't bring it up.

What must it feel like, I wondered, to have the man you'd lived alongside for so long go off and die with some other woman? The only grief I could know right now was the grief of having lost a parent. Mom, in turn, couldn't feel what I felt at having lost Dad as a father.

Given the burden of the loneliness she had to carry, I felt proud of how she was spending her days here: making her way around the shops of Shimokitazawa, talking to people and making connections, as though she was falteringly putting together a new map for herself with each step. It was a strange way of doing it, but it made sense to me. I saw the way she kept her sights on what was real, not living too much in the past or looking too far into the future, and thought, *What a fine woman.*

THAT NIGHT, I DREAMED about Dad.

He was looking for something at the apartment. I'd gone back there for something or other, unlocked the heavy front door and pushed it open. The light was on inside, and I said, "Mom?"

The entry was lined with Mom's shoes—Ferragamo, Gucci, and so on—as well as my Crocs, and Dad's big Converse. I thought about how you could read the history of a family by the shoes in the entryway. A person's shoes waiting there signified that they lived here, that they were still alive.

The light in the entry felt strangely bright.

It came from a small chandelier of Venetian glass that Mom had taken a liking to and splurged on. Its multicolored beams seemed to pierce my eyes.

There was a rummaging sound from inside the condo, and when I tried to peer in, Dad stepped quickly into the entry.

"Oh, Yocchan, it's you," he said. "I thought it might be Mom."

"Isn't she around?"

"No."

"I think she's in Shimokitazawa."

"Shimokitazawa?" A cloud passed over Dad's face, and he looked a little sad.

"What are you doing here yourself? I thought you said were going to be staying at the recording studio tonight," I said.

"I was, but I couldn't find it, so I came back to look."

"For what?"

"My cell phone. Thought I'd give Mom a call."

"Oh, your phone," I said. I wanted to add, *I'll help you look*, but I couldn't make my mouth form the words. I desperately wondered why.

Wait, his cell phone . . . I had a feeling it was gone, but I couldn't remember what had happened. The thought brought a lump to my throat. I wasn't sure why, when I just wanted to help him find it, without worrying about why it was lost.

I looked down at my feet, feeling defeated and angry, and tears of frustration sprang from my eyes. All I wanted to say was *Let me help*, but I couldn't make the words come out of my mouth. It was as though someone had their hand around my throat.

Don't search alone, Dad, turn around and look at me, I thought. But he just kept looking for his phone with his back to me.

I woke up at dawn, feeling forlorn.

I wasn't crying, but my hands were balled into fists under the covers.

Beside me, Mom was sleeping soundly. I saw the rounded shape of her back, and the line of her spine rising from it. Reassured, I went back to sleep.

It was around then that I met Shintani-kun.

I was getting used to the flow of life with Mom and the rhythm of work at the bistro. Enough that I was able to clear up after closing with a glass of wine in hand, or to remember what needed prepping for the next day's service without referring to my notes.

"Are you still serving? I'm on my own. May I sit at the bar?"

When he stepped into the bistro—glasses, strong legs, somehow obviously a music fan but not punk or a rocker, fair-skinned, square jaw, well-dressed and clean, but on first impression somehow a little somber—I was sure, just for a moment, that it was him.

Dad? What are you doing here?

But when I looked more closely, the customer looked nothing like him. At a stretch, if I had to find a point of resemblance, the customer might have had a slouch that was slightly reminiscent of Dad's.

"We'll be taking last orders in ten minutes. Please take a table, if you'd prefer," I said.

"Thanks, I will," said the customer. It was his voice, I realized, that reminded me of Dad—resonant yet soft, and slightly hoarse. I wished he'd open his mouth again and say something else.

He ordered a glass of champagne and the pork rillettes with bread, and ate with almost swoon-worthy eagerness. Not mechanically, but heartily, and with obvious enjoyment. I'd never seen anyone eat so well, I thought. The only person who came close to eating with as much grace and fluency was the critic Kei Kurusu, whom they called the King of Epicures. Come to think of it, the customer resembled him a little, too.

He spent half an hour over his meal, and didn't linger afterward.

When he said *Thank you* on his way out, I closed my eyes to savor the echo of his voice. A fine voice, I thought, a familiar-feeling voice.

As a customer, he certainly made an impression on me.

Coming alone to a place like this—he's probably vetting it for a date with his girlfriend, I thought.

But the next time he came in, he was still alone. Like the first time, he arrived just before closing, and had a plate of couscous and a glass of red wine, and left.

How to express the attractiveness of the way he ate? It was like watching a tea ceremony. Each movement leading to the next, no gesture wasted. Not rushed, not dragging. But with a sense of forward motion.

My boss Michiyo-san thought so, too. The third or fourth time the customer came in, she said, "The way he eats is really satisfying. I mean, it's pretty motivating to cook for."

Leave it up to Michiyo-san, I thought, to keep tabs on what went on in the dining room even though she was in the kitchen most of the time. The customer usually had a glass of wine—red, white, or champagne—and a main course, with bread. He hardly ever went for dessert, or tea or coffee.

Working in food service could be strange in that you were constantly watching people eat. After a while of doing it every day, I started being able to read someone's appetite, or even their personality, in the way they ate their meal. I slowly gained a feel for the right time to approach a table, and the kind of service they might appreciate. At the beginning, I used to work my way down a mental checklist, but gradually, I found I could sense how my customers were feeling. Things like *That person wants more water*, or *They're not finished with that cup of tea*, or *I should offer them another drink*.

I was smitten by the process of acquiring this new understanding.

The satisfaction of doing something over and over, by rote, until one day you saw something differently. It felt like working on listening comprehension in English class at school, and suddenly realizing you actually understood what was being said.

I knew, vaguely, that just as the world contained forces that nurtured and strengthened and created things, there were also forces that diminished them. And that even though there were equal amounts of both, the latter could sometimes seem more powerful.

But as a woman—I was no longer a girl, albeit still a fledgling—I had the power to ignore the force that diminished. To treat it as though it didn't exist, in the same way I washed dirt off potatoes, or pulled weeds from the garden. I could use my body to keep tapping into the opposite force.

Each time Shintani-kun came to the bistro, I observed him, trying to figure out exactly what I found so compelling in the way he ate. I held the feeling close to my chest, a small pleasure to cradle.

Of course, the pleasure was entirely secret. If I ever told a customer, especially someone on their own, *I love the way you eat!*—chances were they'd never set foot in the restaurant again.

Shintani-kun often brought a book to read while he waited, but he'd close it as soon as his food arrived. I liked that too. As well as the way he always said *Itadakimasu*, quietly, before he started eating.

Maybe I was already in love.

ONE LATE AFTERNOON, I came back to the apartment on my break. Mom was nowhere to be seen, so I decided to head toward the coffee shop about halfway down the main street of shops on the east side of Shimokitazawa Station, for coffee beans and a latte to go. It was a long-established store called Maldive, where the owner roasted coffee in a machine that sat right there on the shop floor. The incredible fragrance floated down the whole street of shops as he operated the machine with his muscular arms, just as he had done for decades. It always inspired me to enjoy my cup of coffee and make the most of the day.

It was fall, and the cold air was settling in.

I touched the trunk of the cherry tree that stood on the corner where the bistro was, and walked toward the main street of shops. I remembered how in spring, when the tree was in full bloom, the pink of the blossoms set off the brown walls of the bistro, and enveloped the whole corner with a sweeter, pleasurable air. Passersby would raise their heads to see the flowers as they walked past and smile, like moviegoers looking up at a screen showing a happy film.

In spring, it was hard work keeping the sidewalk outside the shop clear of fallen petals, but I loved the tree and didn't begrudge the work. A long time ago, I happened to visit Shimokitazawa when it was in full bloom, and had been dazzled by the sight. Since then, I'd laid my hand on its trunk each time I passed by, whether it was in leaf, or bare in winter. The habit had become one of the many daily points of contact that anchored me to life in this town.

I passed the corner with the cherry tree, and carried on into the main street.

I was in Maldive, clutching my bag of Mom's favorite beans, an organic coffee from Ecuador, and waiting for my latte, when Shintani-kun walked in.

"Hello," he said, seeing me.

"Hello," I said, thinking it could hardly be called a surprise that we'd run into each other here. I smiled the same smile I used at work when he came into the bistro.

He bought some beans, and I found myself making a mental note: *You brew your coffee in a filter machine with a single-hole dripper, and enjoy the acidity of the Kona.*

"Um," he said, turning to me abruptly. "Um, I'm sorry if I'm mistaken. But are you the daughter of Mr. Imoto? From the band Sprout?"

I cried out in surprise, loud enough for the owner of the coffee shop to raise his head from the roaster. "Yes, I am. You know him?" I said.

"I'm sorry for your loss," he said. "My name's Shintani. I work at a venue where your dad and his band played regularly."

"Oh, right! That must be the one in Shinjuku?"

"That's the one."

"You like music, then," I said.

"I'm not an expert on the grown-up, British-influenced kind of rock that Sprout played, but I love domestic indie bands. We get a lot of them playing at our venue, too. The first time I ended up at your restaurant, I'd just been to a show at Lady Jane, around the corner. I knew I recognized you from somewhere, and then I remembered seeing you and your mother backstage once, when you were looking for your father," he said.

"Oh, I see. I know the band had a regular night at your venue for a long time. I'm sorry they had to quit, with my dad dying in such a terrible way . . ."

"About that—there's something I wanted to tell you," he said.

"What do you mean?"

"I was really unsure about this," he said. "But I'm pretty good at remembering people's faces, and knowing when I've met someone before. That's also why I recognized you."

"I wish I had that skill. I'm sure you'd be good at running a shop," I said, recalling how when I'd started at the bistro, I'd had to resort to sketching cartoons of the regulars so I could remember their names.

"I do," he said. "The venue was actually founded by my father, and I manage it now." He smiled. His teeth were slightly, endearingly crooked.

"Oh, I'm sorry, I didn't realize. That's impressive, for someone your age."

"It just got handed down to me. No different from being the son of a fishmonger or something."

WE'D BEEN DRINKING OUR coffee in the niche with the wooden barrel that served as a table, but more customers were coming in and out to buy beans and coffees, and the place was getting crowded. We agreed to move somewhere we could talk more quietly, and said good-bye to the owner and left the shop.

"Where would you like to go?" he said.

"We've just had coffee, so what about going to Chaka Theka for a cup of chai?" I said, wondering why this man was so easy to talk to. Was it because he reminded me of Dad? I liked how he didn't smile too much as he talked, and spoke carefully, without dropping the ends off his words.

"I've never been there. I'd love to try it," he said.

CHAKA THEKA WAS ON the other side of the tracks, down a small side street that we turned into through the throng of people by the shop that sold roasted rice cakes. The casual restaurant was run by the manager-chef, Tanaka-san, who served home-cooked ethnic food from different cuisines. Mom, whose digestion still wasn't up to anything too heavy, swore by the food here, which sat easily in the stomach. When we ate out on my days off, we often walked over the tracks to this little eatery.

In the late afternoon, after lunch service, they served truly delicious spiced chai, and a signature banana cake. Shortly after Mom had moved in, she'd had a slice of the banana cake and been so taken with it that she'd asked Tanaka-san to bake extra so we could take it home for a housewarming celebration. We'd feasted on cake with whipped cream, and beer, in place of dinner.

Tanaka-san was quiet and could seem intimidating, but behind that exterior lay a passionate and empathetic soul. When Mom had explained how she'd ended up moving to the neighborhood, Tanaka-san had given Mom the whole cake, when she'd only asked for half, and had gifted it to her free of charge.

At the time, I was still so shrunken into myself I couldn't quite believe what was happening. I'd never dreamed that Mom and I could ever do anything as fun as gorging on an entire cake until our bellies ached. We weren't being hysterical, or depressed. We'd just thought of something nice to do, and done it together.

That kind of thing had felt wrong in Meguro, but the new apartment somehow made it possible.

Tanaka-san wasn't in just then, so we asked the part-time waitress for a smoking table near the door. *Oh, right, this isn't a date,* I thought, feeling a little deflated. I was here to spend my break hearing some heavy news about Dad from when he'd been alive.

"I apologize if this is unwelcome," Shintani-kun said.

"Oh, no, please," I said, "I want to know everything about him. Anything."

"Then I'll tell you. Did you see the photo of the woman who died with him, in that magazine? The sort of melancholic beauty?"

"Yes. I didn't want to look very closely, but I think that only made me remember her more clearly," I said.

"I saw her at our venue, just once," he said.

"What?" I was surprised, since from what I'd heard, no one in Dad's circle had known about her.

"She didn't stand out, or call attention to herself. It was almost like she was barely there, but for some reason she made an impression on me. It bothered me so much, I asked Yamazaki-san, who played drums in your father's band, about her. And he said he thought he might have seen her, too. I asked the others, too, just casually, but none of the others did, just us.

"I don't know why, but she was the kind of woman who gave you chills just to look at her. And as you know, Sprout played at the venue every month, but I can say with almost complete certainty that she was never back after that. I don't know whether or not your father spoke to her that night—I think it would have been about a year before they died. Did anyone else know she'd been there?" he asked.

"No, I don't think so. Not Mom, or the police," I said.

"I know it doesn't change the fact that she started a relationship with your father at some point after that, and since they both died, it won't come to criminal charges. But I thought it would give a different picture of things if the family—you and your mother—were to know this. So I wanted to make sure you did. Even though I know it's hardly my place to be raking it back up," he said.

"I wonder why Dad never introduced her, or even mentioned her, to Yamazaki-san. They were close," I said.

"Yamazaki-san told me your father had come to ask for his advice on something. But he didn't make the connection between that strange woman and the one who died. He'd forgotten all about her until we spoke—that was when he first thought of it. And he said your father had asked him not to tell you and your mother about the woman he was seeing, he was sure of that.

"That's why he didn't feel able to tell you about this. He said it would be fine for me to, if I had a chance, since I was the one to notice. Yamazaki-san plays in other bands that play at our venue, too, so I see him often. He seemed to think it might be better to let things lie, since telling you wasn't going to change anything, so long after it happened. So me telling you now is in some ways a bit of a self-indulgence," he said.

His story was saturated with the familiar and condensed essence of Dad's old life.

I gazed out the window at the private road that led to the restaurant. On the main street, a steady stream of young people was passing. The street was decorated with colorful streamers that waved in the wind and gave the street the air of a festival in Nepal or Thailand.

"It doesn't matter, anyway, now he's not here anymore," I said, impetuously. "But I'm glad to learn something I didn't know. Thank you."

"Well, like I said, I know it doesn't mean much. I just thought, if it was me, I'd like to know," he said, a little apologetically.

"We heard from the police that Dad and that woman were actually distant relatives. His younger sister got married to a man in Ibaraki, and that woman was her husband's . . . niece? I think. We only saw my aunt every once in a while, and she hadn't even ever met the woman.

"They told us that when he died, he had quite a lot of alcohol in his system, even though he was intolerant to booze and never drank. I guess he was pretty nervous about something they were going to talk about? I don't know what. Maybe money. The police let us know that the woman wasn't pregnant," I said, looking down at my hands wrapped around the cup of spiced chai.

"I wish now I could have done something that night," Shintani-kun said. "There was something about that woman that really bothered me. I couldn't put my finger on it, but it was troubling and stuck in my memory. It was like she had a darkness that could exert some kind of influence over people. That night might have been the first time that she spoke to your father. I kept thinking—*If only I'd told you, or Yamazaki-san about it earlier*—even though I know there's no way I could have done. That's why I kept coming to the restaurant. But I was never able to broach the subject, and I thought it was none of my business, since it wasn't going to change anything that had already happened.

"And the food was good, and you looked happy working there, and lately I'd been telling myself I could let it be. So if I hadn't run into you earlier, I might not ever have brought it up.

"You look so happy, when you're at work. I always enjoy seeing it. You just go about things in such a satisfying way—always going straight for the jobs most people would avoid. Actually, I even wondered whether you'd like to come work for us. Not that I've come here to headhunt you," he said, and smiled.

I blushed. *He noticed me*, I thought. But I could hardly confess that I liked the way he ate, too.

In spite of his delicate appearance, I could tell from his words and the way he spoke them that he was purposeful person. I liked him even more knowing that he wasn't just a spoiled young privileged gourmet.

My heart was fluttering in my chest. At the same time, another me inside the me who'd been acting strong for Mom—a childlike me—felt confused and sad, and started acting up. All I wanted was to see Dad just one more time, and ask him what had happened. But that was impossible, and I could never know. The regret and the defeat and the lingering sense of injustice all came rushing back.

Out of nowhere, a tear rolled down my cheek and fell onto my slice of banana cake. I hurriedly wiped my eyes with my sleeve.

He took my hand firmly. "I'm really sorry. I keep telling you things I have no business saying," he said.

I felt like I could the sound of his heart beating.

"I don't know anything about you—just what you're like when you're working. I don't know if you have a boyfriend, whether you live with someone, anything. But I feel like I'm losing track of why we're here, because I'm desperate to find out, to know more about you. I want you to know I wasn't using your father as an excuse for us to talk. But at some point I started to look forward a lot to eating at the restaurant, and I knew I had it backward, but it became harder and harder to tell you, and I started feeling like I had an ulterior motive," he said.

I do live with someone, I thought, as he said it, *but it's my Mom.* I was baffled as to how the conversation had taken this sudden turn.

"No, it's fine," I said, my voice nasal from crying. I was looking down at my feet, and his big sneakers next to them, too embarrassed to look him in the eye. "That's all fine. Thank you for telling me."

"I'm glad you don't mind," he said. As he did, I saw that his face had gone bright red, and I thought I would like to get to know him better. Next time, when I wasn't on my afternoon break, and didn't desperately need to blow my nose.

WHEN I CASUALLY MENTIONED it to Michiyo-san, she smirked knowingly, and treated me to a freshly squeezed orange juice.

"I had a feeling he was interested in you," she said.

When I got home after my shift, Mom was still out. I lay down on the floor, looked up at the wood grain on the ceiling, and thought.

I decided to talk to Yamazaki-san when I got the chance, without telling Mom. I felt like everything was moving quickly, that things were changing all at once, and that there was lots to be done.

I dozed off.

I dreamed that someone was calling out to me.

In the dream, I was at the condo in Meguro. Indirect lighting illuminated the hallway. *Wait,* I thought. *Am I alone? Do I live here?* I noticed myself wondering, and thought it was strange. Deep down, I had a nagging feeling I'd left Mom behind somewhere.

Dad? I asked, and searched for him through the condo. He wasn't there. Nor was the photo of him we'd put up after the funeral.

The sounds I was making echoed through the silent apartment, loud and clear, like footsteps echoing down a long hallway.

Where's the photo? We put it here, and not on the family altar, so we could have him close by. Is he still alive, in this dream? I wondered. *If I wait here, will he come back?* I walked into the living room. Mom had always had a vase of cut flowers on the dining table, which was attached to the kitchen worktop, but in the dream there were no flowers. *Mom's not here anymore,* I thought.

On the table there was a newspaper.

It was open to an article. It was bigger than it had been in real life—I guessed that was because it was a dream. It was the size of a full-page ad.

There was a photo of Dad, and of that woman.

The article beneath it ran, *Mitsuharu Imoto, keyboard player of Sprout, a cult rock band which appealed to young and mature audiences alike, committed suicide with a woman . . . The band had appeared at such and such events with so-and-so . . .*

Above it, there was a large photo of that woman. She had small, slight features, a slender face. A woman with wavy hair in a side parting, who looked nothing like Mom, who was like a mirage.

When I saw her face, I was struck by an inexpressible terror. *This woman has tried to die with other men as well*, I thought. *Her eyes say so. Is she satisfied now, having killed Dad? I have to make sure*, I thought. In my panic I felt confused. Some kind of force was trying to pull me down into a dark place, and I felt it filling the room.

This woman hasn't got any of the things I think are important. That makes her invulnerable. She could defeat me instantly.

The things I believed in were puny and insignificant in the face of a power like this—that was why Dad had died. And the world was full of dark forces like that. In the terrifyingly vast entirely of existence, which contained everything conceivable, there seemed to be no use in me trying to speak up and say anything at all. Even if deep down I was connected to the whole of it, any thought that I could contain in my head was bound to be ineffectual and pointless.

Where's the phone? I need to call someone, tell Mom. I panicked and floundered in my dream. I moved the newspaper aside, and there was Dad's cell phone. *He was looking for this,* I thought, and reached for it.

"You'll catch cold dozing off like that," I heard Mom say. She was putting a blanket over me.

"What? Where am I? This isn't Meguro?" I said, confused. "Where's the phone? Dad's cell? I found it, but where did it go? He asked me to."

"You're still half asleep. It's one o'clock! Go to bed, if you're going to sleep," Mom said. Her cheeks were pink, and she looked like she'd had a few drinks. The bags under her eyes made her look endearingly middle-aged. A strange, tender feeling came over me, and I wanted to hold onto her and lick her like a kitten. This was how Mom was going to grow old, I thought. And Dad was missing it.

"Who have you been out drinking with?" I asked.

"I was just talking to Chizuru, at her bar. The cool underground place with the huge lizard on the ceiling? Chizuru's older than me, but she's got a sexy voice, and she's so laid back, and responsible, and generous, and wow, I'm kind of envious. I want to be more like her when I get older," Mom said.

"There wasn't any juicy gossip, or anything. I don't think I even remember how to fall in love anymore. Every time I get remotely excited about anything, I feel like I'm going to be punished. I live frugally, but when I'm out drinking, I start fretting about running out of money."

"I know what you mean," I said. Mom nodded, and went to wash her face.

I didn't mention Shintani-kun.

Mom could be surprisingly oblivious to that kind of thing. When I was a student, there was one time I had a fairly long-term boyfriend, but until we ran into her on a date in Jiyugaoka, she hadn't had a clue. Even then, she just kind of smirked knowingly about it, and didn't quiz me about him or tell Dad.

I was of two minds about telling Mom about that woman.

The other me inside me wanted to go to her and cry, and ask her what to do, tell her everything and make a big fuss, and run away and go to sleep.

But the present me—the me who had strange dreams, the grown-up me who had a job and the basics of a life—there was a spark inside me that said, *Keep quiet for now. Not telling her isn't a betrayal.* It said, *Wait until you know more. Leave her in peace for even just a second longer . . .*

WHEN I WOKE UP the next day, I was surprised by the sight of Mom making omelettes.

The morning light shone on the tatami matting and roused a comforting, musty kind of scent that mixed in with the smell of melting butter.

I thought of a time when I was a young child, before I had my own room at home. Dad slept in another room, ostensibly because he was always back late, and Mom slept with me. Had they not been having sex at that point? I wondered. Maybe their relationship had been sexless even once I was older and had my own room. Had Mom ever had a boyfriend? I was too scared to ask her, yet, but I wanted to sometime.

My old room had been next to the kitchen, and when I woke up, I could always see Mom's back as she made breakfast with the door open so I didn't get lonely.

Mom had just been doing what she did every day, without any special kindness or warmth. So why had it felt so safe? How had it made me feel as though there was no such thing in this world as war, no murder, no betrayal, no robbery, no rape? How had I been able to feel like the world was full of good people? Granted, I still hadn't ever directly been hurt by anyone who wished me ill. But I knew now, in a visceral way, that things could happen in the world that were too awful to believe.

It was bad enough having your father go off and commit suicide with some strange woman, but on top of that, I pitied myself for having become used to it, for accepting it as a part of my life. Back then, I hadn't had an inkling of anything like that. I'd assumed that both Mom and Dad would live and look after me forever.

"'Morning, Mom," I said.

"Oh, you're awake?" she said. "I don't know why, but I was really hungry. I'll make you one, too."

"Thanks, I'll be up in a minute," I said, and roused myself from the futon.

For some reason, it was easier to get up in the mornings now, in this small apartment, than it had been to get up out of my bed in Meguro. In spite of the traffic noise just outside the window, and the sun streaming in from between the curtains which stopped you sleeping in, unlike the blackout-lined drapes that had protected my sleep in Meguro. Despite the lack of a security system or auto-locking front door, or the fact that Mom and I were living together because Dad was gone.

Our life now had its own kind of wide-open contentment, like how it felt to be camping and sleeping in a tent.

"I know it's pretty cramped here, and I feel bad about taking up more space, but do you mind if I get a planter for the windowsill?" Mom asked.

"Sure, why?" I said.

"I was thinking of growing some basil, and cilantro, and rosemary and stuff, things I could put in an omelette, for example," she said.

"Wow, then I could even take some in to the bistro," I said.

"If they end up doing okay. But if you're happy with the idea, I'll go shopping later, for seedlings and whatnot," she said.

"I thought you had to wait until spring for seedlings?" I said.

"Could be. But you never know. There might be seeds maybe, or mint. I'm sure this window gets enough sun to make it work," Mom said, her enthusiasm undaunted by unseasonableness.

"That's true," I said. I was just happy to see her excited about something, so I didn't particularly care about the details.

"That means I'll have to be here until spring, at least. I don't know why I never thought of it in Meguro, even though I was doing a lot more cooking there," she said quietly.

"Maybe it's because you're having fun?" I said.

"Even though Dad's not here?" she said.

"Maybe it's set you free." I smiled.

"Could be. But maybe I was kind of half dead, back then. And Dad too, in a way. Not that Meguro was the problem. There are plenty of people who really enjoy their lives there. I mean, take those people you see on Marie Claire Street in Jiyugaoka during the goddess festival! The look so happy, you wonder if they're quite right in the head. Checking out the street stalls with a glass of wine in hand, picnicking with their families, and all that," Mom said.

"You're right. I guess it's not that Shimokitazawa's special," I said.

It was true that Meguro was exciting in its own way. An intellectual atmosphere prevailed there, as though it was full of people who'd only started trying to figure out how to enjoy life once they'd grown up and established responsible lives. And in the backstreets, there were old-fashioned Chinese restaurants and bars, and people from all different walks of life seeking different things. It wasn't full of young people or tourists, like Shimokitazawa. I recalled a lot of well-heeled ladies, and very young children.

"But it's strange," Mom said. "Back then, it never would have occurred to me to sit down on a bench on Marie Claire Street with a glass of wine and watch the people walk past. I was always rushing, feeling like I needed to be doing something. Emotionally, I was always strapped.

"This neighborhood reminds me of Yanaka, where we lived for a bit after we got married, when you were a baby. That area has a housing allowance for newlyweds, that was why. We rented a little apartment so we could put some money aside. That's why I have fond memories, I guess. Back then both your Dad and I were happy, for no particular reason—maybe because we were young, or it was just that kind of age. We'd shop every day in Yanaka Ginza—we'd get deli food for dinner, savory preserves, roasted rice crackers, and then a cup of tea. If we had time, we'd stop at the traditional dessert parlor and have a beer, or some *isobeyaki*," she said.

"I don't understand how you got from there to being half dead, or—in Dad's case—actually dead," I said. I was worried by the thought that it might happen to me, too, once I got married and had children, grew older and less fit, or got busy with work. I imagined how those things must pile up little by little, until suddenly you noticed that you were totally hemmed in.

"The grime and the haze of being in the world weighed us down, I guess? I know that wasn't all. I think I got further and further away from myself, and lost sight of what I wanted to do,"

Mom said, with a faraway look in her eyes. She lifted the pan and plated up my omelette, and said, "But I know those are just excuses. I'm doing it right this time. That's my only revenge, and the only thing I can do to honor his memory."

When she said that, I suddenly wanted to shout: *Mom!*

Instead, I covered my face and started to cry.

"There's no need to cry. Look, here's your omelette," Mom said, without looking at me, just like she'd done when I was a child. She had a funny habit, at emotional moments, of passing straight through embarrassment into downright coldness. Dad and I had often talked about how contrary she could be.

I wiped at my tears and ate my omelette. It was warm, with plenty of parsley, and tasted of cheese. It was a familiar flavor I'd known in childhood. *Remember, you still have to go to work,* I thought. *Don't let your customers see you've been crying. Hold yourself together,* I told myself, and dried my eyes.

SHINTANI-KUN TURNED UP AT the bistro again a few weeks later, looking slightly self-conscious.

We hadn't even exchanged numbers.

I'd been working hard that day and was covered in sweat. When I spotted him, I was momentarily embarrassed to be so wilted, but actually, even that brought back a welcome memory— the feeling you got from someone having come to find you, a sensation you could only remember when you were in love, which made you feel like nothing bad could happen—something I could only describe as peace.

Shintani-kun had sat down at the bar, as usual, taken off his iPod earphones, and ordered the confit duck with a glass of white.

I suddenly realized that I didn't know him at all. The things that had shaped his life until now, or the things he hoped for in the future—anything. My emotions quickly cooled, and I remembered that I was at work. I'd never felt comfortable with restaurants where the regulars hogged the seats at the bar and monopolized the staff. I wanted to make the bistro a place where all our customers could feel welcome, which meant I couldn't be overfamiliar with Shintani-kun. I made an effort to act the same around him, and only Michiyo-san, who'd caught wind of what was going on, had a smile for me every time I went back to the kitchen to fetch a dish.

"Would you like to leave with me? I'll walk you home," Shintani-kun said casually, when I brought his coffee at the end of his meal.

"Okay, but . . . you don't know, do you? I only live a minute from here. I'm not even heading to the station," I said, and pointed out the window. My apartment was brightly lit up inside, meaning Mom was already home. Its romantic potential was severely limited.

"Do you want to go for a drink, then?" he said.

"Can you give me thirty minutes? I have to clear up," I said.

"Of course. I'll meet you at the wine bar on Azuma Street," he said.

"See you there," I said. We talked like we'd known each other for a long time, but I had to remember that we hadn't. I vowed that whatever happened with Shintani-kun, I would never use Dad as an excuse to spend more time with him. Dad might have brought Shintani-kun into my life for me, but from now on, I would square away whatever I discovered about his death on my own.

Closing up took longer than I thought, and it was forty-five minutes later that Michiyo-san sent me out the door with a knowing smile. I hadn't been about to cut corners on cleanup or prep just because I had something like a date. I found Shintani-kun perched on a stool reading a book, eating cheese and drinking a glass of red wine.

"I've kept you waiting. Sorry I'm late," I said.

"I understand," he said. "It was a sudden invitation, anyway."

We didn't have anything in particular to talk about aside from Dad, so we talked about music. But the Japanese indie bands that Shintani-kun liked, which actually leaned more toward the dance music end of the spectrum than the rock end, were an enigma to me. My musical education had consisted of a smidgen of jazz, and a sampling of UK and American classic rock. Plus, growing up in a house where there was always music playing, I'd never bothered to put names to the songs I was listening to.

"So, Yoshie, who's your all-time top secret celebrity crush?" Shintani-kun asked.

"Hmm, if I had to choose? I'd have to go for Paddy McAloon," I said, which fell totally flat, because Shintani-kun had no idea who I was talking about.

Unfortunately, it simply wasn't in my character to follow up and patch over this kind of conversational lapse. I was aware that this was a trait of mine that men often took advantage of by assuming whatever they liked about me, and therefore found attractive, but sadly I'd always been that way. I was tired from being at work all day, and this was an impromptu evening, and I didn't want to have to make too much effort. I did enough of that at work. *I just want to have a drink and enjoy myself,* I thought, and proposed a carafe of a nice white.

"Drinks taste better in Shimokitazawa," I told him. "You watch the people going past outside, and they look so relaxed, and happy, even though they don't even live here. There aren't that many places like this in Tokyo."

"Yes, I agree, I really think so. Everyone looks youthful, too. Somewhere like Ginza, people look more tired. Although that can be nice, too," he said, and smiled. It was like seeing a cat stretch.

His words moved me again, just a little. *There's another thing I like about him,* I thought, *aside from the way he eats,* and I decided to spend some more time like this, finding more.

By THE TIME I finally contacted Yamazaki-san, the drummer, Shintani-kun and I had been out several times. I'd been putting it off through being busy, and not knowing where to start with the whole thing, until one day I was off work, and finally got up the nerve to give him a call.

The main reason was that when Shintani-kun had mentioned him, I'd realized I wanted to see Yamazaki-san again. I hadn't seen him since Dad's private funeral—Dad's band had broken up, so there were no more gigs. Yamazaki-san had always been around, and suddenly I didn't see him anymore. So I missed him.

I was pretty sure Yamazaki-san had been Dad's closest friend. Dad had had a wide circle of friends and acquaintances, as wide as the range of music he did, but I think Yamazaki-san was the only one he ever really opened up to.

Yamazaki-san was a lot younger than Dad, but he looked far older than he was. Mom and I joked that he looked like the TV detective Lieutenant Columbo, and started calling him that when I was a child. Sometimes, he'd turn up in a trench coat, just like the detective, and Mom and I would look at each other and smile.

He was well built and tall, and his clear, round, puppy-dog eyes were light brown. His hair, too, was light brown and fluffy, and curled high on his head, and he always went on stage in his normal clothes. According to Dad, Yamazaki-san was quite particular about the color and style of his clothing, and refused to wear things he didn't feel comfortable in. That explained why he always seemed to be wearing the same thing.

He also had an unbelievably beautiful wife—so much that when she turned up at their gigs, both the band and the audience would get all unsettled. Mom used to say, "Her beauty outshines even mine." Secretly, I thought they weren't even in the same league. She was so slim, beautiful, and graceful in every movement and gesture, she put me in mind of the classic movie stars from the sixties, like Ayumi Ishida or Ruriko Asaoka. Rumor had it that she'd once been a model, and also that Yamazaki-san had fallen for her at first sight and courted her for a long time before she finally agreed to marry him.

When I spotted him approaching 3.4, an old-fashioned tea shop in Shibuya around the back of Tokyu Hands, I suddenly remembered how I often used to wait here for Dad, back when I was in high school. My chest felt tight at the memory.

I'd be feeling reluctant about having promised to meet up with him, feeling like maybe we didn't have much to talk about because of our age difference, and questioning whether I wanted to be there, but then I'd catch sight of his face and feel glad to have gone through with it, after all.

It's no good, I thought. *There's no use me doing anything with anyone right now—I'm living in Dad's shadow, like someone who's just had their heart broken. I keep looking for him, because he's the one who's on my mind.* I feared I might have to live with this condition for the rest of my life. That was a prognosis I was hardly prepared for. What a mess I was in! There was no way of knowing whether I'd ever make a full recovery.

But I had no time to dwell on these thoughts. I was nervous, but seeing as I had asked Yamazaki-san to meet me, it was my job to ask questions.

"Hi, Yocchan. What's going on? What did you want to talk to me about?" Yamazaki-san said, gulping down his drink, the strongest coffee on the menu.

I was drinking a spicy ginger tea with fresh grated ginger on the side. The shop smelled of the sturdy wood of the old, well-polished chairs and tables, dry dust, and old books. Goldfish swam slowly in a round bowl. It was a tea shop, of Dad's and Yamazaki-san's generation, not a café. It felt cozy and comforting like something from of my childhood.

"Well, it's about the woman who died with Dad. If there's anything you can tell me, I'd like to know," I said. "I know my father asked you not to tell us. So whatever you feel able to."

It had been a while since I'd talked to a man of his age, and even things like the wrinkles in his jacket and the slightly flabby skin at the back of his neck felt nostalgic and endearing to me. I wanted to breathe in and fill my chest with the familiarity of it.

When I was a child, Dad often had Yamazaki-san around for dinner. I guessed they must both have had more time back then. His beautiful and quiet wife would come, too, and the adults would have a small party. As an only child, I knew nothing that felt safer than falling asleep listening to the happy sounds they were making. The memories came back to me, vivid and wrenching.

"That's tough," said Yamazaki-san. "It's true, Imo asked me not to tell you or your mother, because he didn't want to worry you."

"If worrying's the problem, I don't see how we could do more than we already have done. And anyway, all that's over now," I said.

"In that case, why don't you put it in the past, leave things be? Things have moved on in your lives, haven't they? Isn't it time we started letting Imo settle into our memories?" Yamazaki-san said, quietly.

His expression was one I'd never seen on him before. I suddenly understood—he, too, was grieving, for his favorite, longest-running band, and his best friend.

"Things have moved on, and that's why I feel like he's been left behind," I said. "Right now, Mom's staying with me in Shimokitazawa, and the old place in Meguro is empty. So I think it's up to me to sort things out, but I kind of panic. I get worried that Mom's not worrying about it. But when I try to think about things, I realize I don't understand, and I get nowhere. I thought you might be able to help."

"You and your mother are in fundamentally different positions right now. It's no wonder there are things you're not on the same page about. But I imagine that must feel especially lonely," Yamazaki-san said. We didn't call him Columbo for nothing, I thought. "I heard through the grapevine that your mother had left home and was staying with you. I think it's kindest for you now to just let her stay, without saying too much."

"I think so, too. But I have this funny feeling there's still more I could be doing," I said adamantly.

Yamazaki-san thought for a while in silence. "I know where you're coming from, actually. If I were in your shoes, at your age, I think I'd say the same. There'd be something wrong with you if you were able to keep going like nothing had happened. So if I were you, I'd feel the same—I'd be desperate to do something, to make it better. But nothing's going to bring him back. I think what you have to do is hold on tight and live with that feeling, even if it's wild and rough, and you feel like you're on the verge of giving up. I sometimes wake up thinking, *Wait, aren't we supposed to be rehearsing for our gig this month? Better call Imo and find out,* and then lie there in bed crying," he said, looking at me steadily with his bright, round eyes. *Imo* was what Yamazaki-san always called Dad. Each time he said the name, I felt like Dad was somewhere close by, and my chest tightened.

"I think I understand what you're saying," I said. "Maybe I'm just tired from trying to do it."

Yamazaki-san nodded, and said, "The story was that she was your dad's, ah, younger sister's husband's child, from when he was young?"

"No, I heard she was my uncle's niece," I said.

"Anyway, neither of those is true. She was actually your dad's sister's daughter, whom she gave birth to when she was very young and had to give up. But your grandma didn't tell your aunt that the baby had been adopted. I don't know how she did it—maybe she told her it had died, or just that she was going to take care of it. Either way, your aunt doesn't know about her. Or maybe she knows, but has decided to forget, or pretend she doesn't."

"What?!" I was taken aback. This meant that woman was a much closer relative than I'd been led to believe.

"From what I understand, she was placed with a family, but it was a difficult environment, and she ran away from home quite young. It seems she led a hard life after that, too," he said.

"I wonder if Dad felt sorry for her," I said. "But wait, wouldn't that have made them too closely related? She was his niece, right?"

"I'm sure that was an issue, too. But my suspicion is that they got involved before they realized. They probably only found out after they'd gone too far," he said. "Frankly, she was a disturbing woman. Shintani-kun might have told you, but I saw her, just once. She had this air about her that gave me the shivers, and she was on my mind the whole night, even while I was on stage. Only Shintani-kun and I seemed to feel it, but we wondered whether she wasn't an actual ghost.

"She disappeared after the gig without staying for the party, so I didn't put it together that the woman was her. I had no idea until Shintani-kun told me.

"Aside from that, I vaguely knew your dad was in some kind of trouble, and he did talk to me about it, just a little. He said there was someone he was seeing. He couldn't break it off, he'd lent her money, and there were some complications. But he thought it would turn out all right, and he had absolutely no intention of leaving his family. He was pretty clear on that. And that's the truth."

When I heard that, relief and regret rushed over me, making my head spin. I felt even more helpless, like I'd been sent a confession of love from someone who was already dead.

"I think your dad got sucked in," Yamazaki-san said, "without meaning to. I think there was a part of him that was drawn to things like that. Something that held him back, no matter how warm and loving you and your mom were. But what an idiot he was—He started a family to get away from that kind of thing, only to throw it away again. Never having had kids, of course I can't say for certain, but if I had a daughter like you I'm sure I would have wanted to stay alive to be with you," Yamazaki-san said looking down at his big hands, with their neatly clipped fingernails.

"I'd like to believe he felt that way," I said.

"I think you can be sure of that," he said immediately. "I remember how fondly he always talked about you. He said you were too good for him. In that sense, your dad was an ordinary, run-of-the-mill father. Not one who'd think it was okay to turn to drink and women, and kill himself. I know guys who are like that, and the difference is obvious. But for some reason, those guys survive, and the good ones like Imo end up dead."

It meant a lot to me to hear that from Dad's closest friend.

"But he probably got closer and closer to the danger, felt drawn in. Bit by bit. Convinced himself that nothing bad could happen. Granted, I only saw her once, but she was the kind of woman who could mess with your thinking so badly that you couldn't see her clearly, no matter how hard you looked. I know she was never brought to justice, since she died, too, but I'm sure she would have been given a sentence if she had been. And I would have gladly testified. But even that wouldn't bring him back. What a mess he's left us in.

"The thing is—and I don't mean to be crude—being in a band and playing music together is exactly like having sex with someone, repeatedly.

"You share an invisible, wordless language of the body. For hours. That's why I've been feeling jealous, like someone's stolen my lover. This whole time, wondering why he didn't open up to me more—I can't tell you how much I've reproached myself for assuming he'd come to me if he got in real trouble. For believing he was all right because he didn't," Yamazaki-san said. I saw tears glinting at the corners of his eyes.

Sex with Dad? That's going a little far, I thought, but surprisingly it didn't make me uncomfortable.

Perhaps it was because I'd experienced something slightly similar. The physical experience of living as the three of us, our bodies in the same space: the way we breathed when we passed by each other in the hallway, the touch of our hands when we handed over a glass, the smell of clothes hanging in our closets, the feeling of his leather shoes when I accidentally stepped on them as I left the house, the awareness of someone's presence in a space—that was what family meant. Why—when we'd shared all those things, and happily enough—had Dad felt the need to tear himself away?

Whenever I talked about Dad to people, I made sure to do it lightly, no matter who I was talking to—friends, people who had heard on the news, or neighbors.

I did the same with Yamazaki-san. I was trying to speak in a measured way, and not be overly positive, or too down. Otherwise, I'd start feeling so depressed I'd want to die, too. Sometimes the molten cauldron deep inside me boiled over like lava, and I felt hot and full in my belly, and something would rise through my chest and stop me from breathing. When that happened, I couldn't think about anything pleasant, anything new. But there was no point hitting other people with it (unlike with Mom, with whom I vented often), so I always talked about it with a detached attitude, staying on the surface, not looking straight at it.

But Yamazaki-san's presence, and how easy he was to talk to, and the closeness I felt toward him as someone who'd also shared Dad, and his absence, made all the things I'd been hiding and ignoring in my new life come flooding out.

I slammed my palms down on the table and started wailing. I wrung more tears out of that bottomless well, which never seemed to dry up no matter how much I cried.

Yamazaki-san didn't put his arm around my shoulders, or stroke my head. But he stayed there with me. I felt him being there.

This is ridiculous, I thought. *Crying at men who remind you of Dad. It's like whoring yourself—no different from sleeping with lots of men because you miss him.* But my tears overrode any logic. When I raised my swollen eyes and my snot-stained face, there was Yamazaki-san, with his kind face and tears in the corners of his eyes, waiting.

He patted the back of my hand with an elegant hand, and said, "He was a really good man, and we both miss him now he's gone."

I could only nod.

Pathetic, I thought. I wasn't recovering, just dragging this around. Dawn wasn't coming, regrets couldn't be redeemed, words left unsaid stayed unsaid. It had been nearly two years, and I was still stuck in the same place—and might be forever.

Even so, come tomorrow morning, I'd be kneading bread dough, boiling water, shredding salad vegetables, mopping the floor. My body would know what to do, and I'd smile and greet customers when they came in. That was all I could do.

In the same way that Mom was actively doing nothing, I had to keep doing the only thing I could.

We each had to live our own battles. We could hardly give up and die; and if we had to live, we'd have to rely on what we were made of. When I went in to the bistro tomorrow, the space would give me a little consolation. I'd been there long enough to get sick of the place, and when I was tired it did feel claustrophobic; but its small but perfect kitchen, the crisp figure of Michiyo-san as she stood in it, witnessing the food her hands turned out as though by magic, and bringing them to people and seeing them smile—it all added up inside me, drop by drop, into some kind of strength. People could kill each other, but people could save each other, too.

"I heard she'd attempted suicide with someone else, previously. I really don't know why Imo got involved with someone like that. It must have been bad luck, and bad timing," Yamazaki-san said.

"Dad wasn't the only one, then?" I said. It was just like I'd thought in my dream.

"That's what Imo said. That she'd tried to die with a man before, and failed, and had been in and out of hospital since, something like that. I told him that didn't sound too good, that he should stay away . . . But your dad said, *I'll be fine, I'm not going to kill myself.* I guess he couldn't leave her be," Yamazaki-san said.

"I didn't think Dad was so dumb and foolish," I said, feeling fastidious.

"What happens between a man and a woman has nothing to do with the mind," Yamazaki-san said, seeing right through me. Sometimes he really was just like Columbo.

I stopped in my tracks, and looked at him with eyes still full of tears. "I'm sure that's true. I guess I don't understand it yet," I said.

"I don't understand it all, either, I don't think. But that's how it is. It's not about reason or sense," he said. "You dad had probably given her a substantial amount of money, too. Didn't she have a lot of debt? And you know he'd rather have died than get into debt himself."

That made a lot of sense to me, and I felt wretched, thinking such a small thing had pushed him to it.

When he died, Dad's bank account was nearly empty, and the savings account he'd been building up to start his own studio had also been cleared out.

Dad, you idiot. What about us? I thought—words I'd repeated many times since he'd died. *Wasn't light enough? The warmth of daily life didn't sustain you? Was the allure of what was dark, dirty, cloudy, and shadowed really so strong, once you'd had a taste—once your heart was stained with it, that it was worth your life?*

As we were leaving, Yamazaki-san said, "Imo really loved you, Yocchan. Remember that—even though I'm hardly the one you ought to be hearing it from. Life isn't always a barrel of laughs, but it's not all terrible, either."

When he said that, I felt like Dad was there, and near enough that I expected him to respond. It was like Dad was speaking through Yamazaki-san.

"You're right. I know I'm trying to make sense of things logically, when I can't," I said. "And I know he loved me."

"That's right . . . My old mother's nearly ninety, but each year in spring she still puts up vegetable preserves—cooks them down into *tsukudani* with soy sauce, sweet rice wine, and sugar. And each year, when I taste that familiar flavor, we both know it could be the last time she makes the spring *tsukudani*. But that's just thoughts. When my mother gets a bumper crop of butterbur or prickly ash, she just gets to it, starts cooking, even if it's hard work. She's not thinking about what might happen next year. The great thing about the everyday is that we don't care about next year, as long as the *tsukudani* turns out good this spring. So I let go, too, and instead of getting maudlin over every mouthful, I just say, *Mom, your* tsukudani's *so good, it's the best, I'm so glad I get to eat it again this year, it makes rice taste so good.* And I think there's a case to be made for you finding your appetite for enjoying that kind of happiness. Of course, what happened to Imo was terrible, and it's healthy to grieve. But aren't you letting fear trick you into thinking too rigidly about the time you have now with your mom?" he said.

Something in me lifted, and I felt myself almost dissolving into the joy in what he said. They were the words I'd been waiting for, and they soaked into me, easing both my body and my soul.

I COULDN'T TELL MOM I'd seen Yamazaki-san, let alone what we'd talked about.

I actually considered coming clean, but that night, at the sight of her lolling around on the floor among cushions, humming a tune and reading a manga she'd bought that day from The Village Vanguard—it was a volume of *Marginal*, by Moto Hagio, whom she'd always been a fan of—I faltered and missed my chance.

When I saw her reading manga with her belly out, shedding tears while murmuring, "I understand, of course you want to go back and live in the cave," I was filled up with the thought that this woman hadn't done anything wrong, and didn't deserve any of this.

Yes, Shimokitazawa was a little like a mountain cave in the outlands, where people who found it difficult to keep up with the vagaries of the world could live quietly, as they wanted. Even people who'd been left behind, like me and Mom.

Even though we were confident enough not to pay much attention to what people thought or said, there had been a time when we'd be walking around Jiyugaoka and feel like people were pointing at us and whispering behind our backs—that we were the family of that man who'd abandoned them in a love-suicide.

That was why I didn't tell Mom about what I'd discovered.

But her mother's intuition must have done it for me, because she asked, "Yocchan, has something happened? You seem down. You weren't working today, so what did you get up to? Hey, your next day off, do you want to go to Isetan together, do some shopping, and have lunch? I'll buy you some winter clothes," she said.

"Okay, let's. But we can't live like this forever, right?" I said.

"Why?" she said, blankly.

"I don't know, it seems kind of temporary," I said.

"Well, it is," she said. "But are you my mom? Why are you so responsible?" She smiled. "I mean, if you decide to go and apprentice at another restaurant somewhere, or overseas even, then things would have to change. But we can cross that bridge when we get to it. It's not happening today, or tomorrow; we're talking about the future. Or if you find a husband. But that would be okay, too. You're the only one I have left, so I'll come and live nearby, and help look after the grandchildren. It could be fun," she said.

"Who said I'd be okay with you coming to live nearby?" I said.

"You'll want some help. It's hard for a woman to keep working. Everyone I knew who did that had a breakdown at some point. You'll need a support system, since—knowing you—you're not going to give up work even if you get married or have children," she said.

"Could be," I said. "I'd like to work for Michiyo-san forever, and maybe even take over when she retires; that's how much I look up to her. Well, she's not that much older than me, so I guess I won't need to take over, but whatever happens, I'd like to keep helping her at the bistro. I love her, and her food."

"It's not often that you find someone like that to work for. You should stick with her, whatever it takes," Mom said.

"If that means I need to go and train somewhere else for a few years, I think I will. I don't care what I end up doing at the bistro, whether it's just front of house, or cleaning, or admin—whatever way I can be involved. It's more important to me than wanting to serve my own food," I said.

"You must be pretty serious about this—it wouldn't be like you to share a half-baked idea," Mom said. "Fair enough, because that barley salad was literally life-giving. I was so miserable I wanted to die, and full of cloudy feelings that rolled around inside me like sludge, and totally stuck, and that salad accepted me as I was. I rediscovered my little, precious spark of life inside that salad."

"Thanks, Mom. That's the best possible compliment," I said.

"The way you say that goes to show how much you're a part of the restaurant now," Mom said. "I think it's about time I started something, too. I'm getting bored of strolling around, and I spent way too long as a housewife."

What on earth was she going to do? Work on the checkout at Ozeki, the supermarket? Waitress in a café, or, god forbid, at a late-night bar? Sell vintage clothes?

I wanted to ask, but restrained myself.

Whatever she said she wanted to do, I thought, I had to be supportive. In the early days, when Mom's spirit seemed to have left her body, I couldn't have imagined her expressing a desire to do anything at all.

"Anyway, Yocchan, have you got a boyfriend yet?" she said.

"No, why do you ask?" I said.

"Women's intuition," Mom said. I was impressed.

"There's someone I might be getting closer to, that's all. But it's not quite coming together yet. I think I'm not ready, either," I said.

"Have you got ED?" she said.

"Um, no, for a number of different reasons," I said, "but it might be something similar.

"Whenever I get excited, or have any fun, or start looking forward to something, I can sense another me observing myself from between cold, harsh waves, like the Japan Sea in winter. Right now, exploring things with a man my own age—talking and getting to know each other and feeling like something could happen—feels like a silly and pointless game."

"Oh, I'm feeling that to the max, at my age," she said. "Seriously, I know what you mean. It's not like I want to act like I'm the only one who's been through hard things, or look down on people who haven't. But the things people say just seem so inconsequential."

Our morale was suffering after that conversation, so we decided to head out to a bar five minutes away on Chazawa-Dori. The drinks weren't cheap, so we only went there occasionally to treat ourselves to the fresh fruit cocktails. They were sweet and delicious as something in a dream, and as we sipped at ours under the dim lights at the beautifully polished bar, a feeling of strength seemed to rise from my throat, and the weight on my shoulders felt a little lighter.

I watched Mom pay as we left. From the back, I had the strange impression that she was looking older, but also the same as ever.

It was cold on the street. The smell of winter was faintly in the air. Mom's early winter coat was a dubious black leather trench that she had apparently acquired at Chicago, the vintage clothing shop. It smelled of old leather as I walked beside her. It was a smell characteristic of old things, which I felt I knew from somewhere.

Time passes. The present is the present. I don't want the nightmares to get the better of me. But sometimes, biologically, I just lose. I'm not grown up enough yet to appreciate the view as I fall and lie there, defeated.

Mom walked with small steps beside me, in the wind, looking normal. *I'll always remember the feeling of this happy night, when we walked slowly down Chazawa-Dori on a whim, like travellers,* I thought, tipsily.

"MOSHI MOSHI? HELLO?"

In my dream, I was calling someone. I was in my room in the apartment in Meguro.

Desperately, I kept calling out. If I could get him to pick up, I thought, I could save him. The signal seemed to be unreliable, and I couldn't tell whether or not the line had connected. The phone kept making a strange sound.

"Hello? Dad! Dad!"

I was shouting.

". . . Yocchan?"

I heard his voice.

"Dad!" I said, and burst into tears.

His voice was brimming with genuine and unconditional love. I could tell—that Dad wanted to see me, until the very end. *But wait,* I thought. *I thought I found his cell phone, last time I was here.* I felt confused.

The signal got weaker again, and I couldn't hear what Dad was saying.

Dad! I shouted again as the line popped and crackled.

Maybe it's hard to hear among the trees, I thought in my

dream. Even though it couldn't have made a difference in reality. Then, at the other end of the line, something changed.

I heard a high, scratchy, woman's voice, too faint to make out what she was saying.

I moved the phone away from me with a shiver.

Feeling a sense of dread as though something had entered in through my ear, I shook my head quickly.

"ARE YOU OKAY?" I felt Mom's hand on me.

The force of this palm pressing on me was a good power. Fallible, uncomfortable, odious, and aggravating as it might have been at times, it was a fundamental energy that had held me, nursed me, and nurtured me.

Relieved, I opened my eyes.

"Mom . . ." I said, still crying.

"You kept saying, 'Dad! Dad!'" she said, sadly. She had her hair down, and her silhouette was wavering in the light of the small lamp against the pitch dark of the tatami-matted room.

"I know," I nodded. I couldn't tell her—Mom, who I was going through so much with.

"You still miss him. Of course you do, and I've been so caught up with myself. I'm sorry," she said, and patted my shoulder.

It's not that, I wanted to say, but I couldn't. I was too afraid, too shaken. And if there really still was a connection open to something of Dad, it might not be open to Mom, and it might mean there was something I could do to help him.

Maybe I was still a little off. About as off as Mom, who'd lived with Dad's ghost back at home.

I didn't feel able to convey the feeling of my dream to Mom. It wasn't that I didn't want to. I'd had plenty of that before. But for the first time, I knew that sometimes love meant not being able to tell. And that it inevitably involved the question of trusting myself to tell sometime, when I could.

I didn't know anything about how souls were supposed to leave this world and reach the afterlife, or about offering prayers and ceremonies so the dead could rest in peace. Nor was I interested—my life recently had been concerned with problems like finding the most efficient way to peel potatoes for the pot-au-feu we served for lunch. But I knew I had to do something, that I didn't want Dad to be trapped in that place. What would it take to shift my dreams into something even just a little happier?

"Mom, stop," I said. "You need to find your own life. I like what I have now, and there's still more I can look for, too. But I have these weird dreams. We . . . we've seen a lot of scary things. Like the car in the forest, and . . ."

My throat closed up.

"The bodies." Mom nodded. She said, "What we saw ruined everything. But we're still here. You can't compare yourself with when things were fine or good. It's better to remember how far we've come from the worst time. Then your dreams will be nothing to be scared of."

I looked into her eyes and realized that Mom was separate from me, but going through this with me. I felt safe. The pitiful safety of licking each other's wounds in a low place, and the miserable contentment of not having been left behind—that was the warmth that consoled me now.

DURING THOSE DAYS WHEN I found myself at work serving customers, keeping those murky, unresolved feelings out of sight, seeing Shintani-kun come into the bistro was always a breath of fresh air. It was like coming home after a long day and petting your dog or cat, although I felt guilty about thinking of it this way. When I saw him, I felt like my eyes, my hands—all of me reverted to the old me, and my body breathed a sigh of relief.

It was a sensation like sinking into a tepid bath at exactly the right temperature—no need to get tense or overwhelmed. Or like wading into the ocean in the evening and watching the sun go down in lukewarm water. The tiredness and the tension in your shoulders melting away into clean seawater, and feeling rocked and lulled by the rhythm of the waves, more thoroughly than in any hot spring.

By then, I knew I didn't want to let him go.

But it wasn't because I liked him. I just didn't want to go through losing him. Whether that was love, I couldn't tell.

"The pot-au-feu's back on the menu today," I said. *If he hadn't seen me here, standing tall, working hard, being competent, would he even have liked me?* I wondered, and doubted.

I'd been through too much too intensely recently to feel comfortable calling the paltry flow of feelings between us love. Thus my goal was simply to keep things between us light and pleasant.

"I'll take it, then, please. This is nice, it's like coming home," he said, taking off his coat and taking a seat at the bar.

He says the cutest things, I thought, as I poured his wine. Lately, Michiyo-san had finally laid off the smirking, but had taken to praising me for not neglecting other customers even when my boyfriend was here. *Of course not; this isn't a hostess bar,* I thought. At the same time, I knew it was a testament to her food and the restaurant that customers kept me busy right up to closing time.

Shintani-kun still ate beautifully, and the pot-au-feu disappeared into his mouth with dreamy alacrity. As he ate, he looked out the window peacefully. He always wore nice shoes.

I felt joy. Working at the bistro, Shintani-kun feeling at home there. Seeing my apartment across the street. I knew it wasn't going to last forever—things changed and moved on, and if you thought they could stay the same, they got ruined, like our family had done. Still, I desperately wanted all of this happiness to stay, just the way it was.

If someone I was dating came to pick me up from the restaurant where I worked, the usual thing would be for them to walk me home after my shift. But since I lived literally across the street, there wasn't much walking that Shintani-kun could do, so we usually ended up having a drink somewhere. We'd talk, but not too long, so he could catch the last train back to Shinjuku.

That night was no exception. We headed to a basement *izakaya* near the station, and ordered some side dishes and a small flask of sake.

The *izakaya* was close to closing, but the owner was a friend of Shintani-kun's, and accommodated us happily when we said we only wanted one drink. Stepping inside was like going several decades back in time. The clientele was mostly a generation or two older than us, men and women glowing from drink and rounding off their evenings with dessert. It was another place that was living proof of the diversity in Shimokitazawa, how welcoming it was to so many people.

"I've never met a woman who ate *bakurai* with so much relish," Shintani-kun said.

"I work in food," I said, "I'll eat anything that's good." *Bakurai*—an orange-colored food made of sea pineapple dressed with salted sea cucumber intestine—was a well-known delicacy, and the one they made here was exceptional. It went so well with the sake I was drinking, I felt invigorated. The staff were cheerful, and so alert and lively it made me forget we were underground. It genuinely inspired me to work harder myself, even though at times I got so tired I thought my legs might cramp.

"Hey, Shintani-kun," I said. "I keep seeing my Dad in my dreams."

"Of course you do," he said confidently. I liked that.

"He doesn't seem very happy," I said. "Like he wants to say something, something he needs to say . . . And Mom also says she sees his ghost when she goes back to the condo. Do you believe in that kind of thing? I started thinking, *what if his soul's still hanging around, because he can't get to the afterlife,* and now I can't stop thinking about it," I said.

"Music venues can be quite scary in that way," Shintani-kun said, "and I know some tragic stories. I mean, musicians don't tend to all be able to make a good living and live happily ever after, if you know what I mean. They die from drugs, from drink, from getting sick and not taking care of themselves, or they have to give up music and find different work, or they get into fights and have feuds and make enemies—lots of things. Some groupies kill themselves . . .

"It doesn't happen often, but it does. You hear about them

turning up on stage, musicians seeing dead girls in the audience while they're playing, that kind of thing," he said quietly.

"Terrifying," I said.

"Personally, I'm not sure yet whether I believe in it all, as such," he said. "But if I was in a band, and someone who was a big fan killed themselves, I could understand feeling like they might still be following us around. Maybe thinking you'd seen them. And if a member of the band died, and someone new joined, but when you looked over while you were playing you thought you saw the dead person instead? I can picture that, too. Even if it was only a trick of the mind.

"So what I do is put aside the question of whether it's real or not, and get the place cleansed just in case. We even have a shelf shrine, in the back. You have to, when you run a business, I think. Sometimes I get to feeling like I'm carrying a lot of it on my shoulders—not the spirits themselves, but the responsibility for a space where different people bring in different energies, and keeping it clean, I guess," he said.

"Yes," I said, feeling relieved in a more mundane way. When someone else made the effort to open up, that made it easier to sense the motions of my own heart.

"So I know what you mean," he said. "The important thing is that the people who are alive feel okay about things. More important than trying to serve or help the dead. In that sense, I can see the value in visiting his grave, or going to the scene, if you feel the need."

"To Ibaraki?" I said, surprised. "The forest? That terrifying and heartbreaking place?"

I'd been thinking I'd never even make it back to the lovely aquarium in Oarai, which we'd visited several times as a family years ago. Dad loved going to aquariums, and whenever we took a family trip, he always planned it so he could take one in.

I cast my mind back to that terrible day at Tokyo Station, surrounded by happy people about to set off on or just returned from their travels, people meeting up and finding each other at the promised hour, when Mom and I felt like the only ones there who'd been dropped into pitch darkness, and the summer sun was so bright it seemed to burn us. The day we waited for the bus to take us to Ibaraki to identify his body and claim it.

If only we could jump back in time, to the day when all three of us got on the bus to the aquarium in Oarai, I'd thought. I'd wished it so hard my temples had started to hurt. We were heading to the same place, so why did we have to feel so much pain?

"I could come with you, if you'd like. The venue's doing fine these days, so I can take some time off," Shintani-kun said.

"No, it's okay. I don't even know whether I could do something like that, yet," I said. "But I'll think about it. How do you get a place cleansed?"

"I ask someone from our local shrine, so there's a whole ceremony to it, but I think something like offering flowers would help, too," he said. "Let me think about it. Remember, rituals are more important than we think. Not for the dead, but I think it's the best way to help ourselves accept what happened, and draw a line under it. In my experience, it puts musicians and our venue staff at ease, and stops their feelings from feeding back and dragging on."

"Thanks. I don't feel ready to take that kind of action yet, but I don't want to keep having these awful dreams, so I need to look into it. I've thought about getting counseling," I said.

"Whatever you do, don't rush yourself," Shintani-kun said. "If you do that and try to take shortcuts, it'll come back to you, later."

"How did you get to know all this? You're still young," I said.

"I've been involved in the alternative music scene since I was young, and I've seen a lot of tragic things, things that don't feel right. You meet so many people, but you say good-bye to so many of them, too. We're a venue with a long history, but small; the kind of people who play with us haven't made it big yet, or aren't ever going to, or have and come back for old times' sake— by which I mean we're the kind of place acts pass through in the course of their careers. There are some groups that are stable and play with us regularly, like your Dad's, which is reassuring, but they're the exception," he said. "I'm an ordinary man, without any talent. But I've seen much more than I can tell."

"That's why you're so grown-up," I said.

"When you've seen so much that's chaotic, you feel drawn to things that are distinct, and certain. Like you, Yocchan," he said.

"You mean, when you've been gazing at muddy swamps you get blinded by the beauty of a lotus flower?" I laughed.

"I'm not sure I'd go that far," Shintani-kun said, and laughed. "I listened to Prefab Sprout, the band you like. I like them a lot, too. Is that where the name of your Dad's band came from?"

"I wonder. I never really asked. But I know he liked them, and he played their records a lot at home. Maybe they've been an influence—their use of female backing vocals is similar, for example. Some of their CDs are out of print now, but I can lend them to you if you'd like," I said.

My heart felt warm.

It was a warmth that the town, and the atmosphere in the *izakaya*, had given me space to hold.

The tone of the energy that flowed through the bar, probably unchanged over the years it had been in existence—the unobtrusive but priceless foundation that its owner and the staff, along with their customers, had spent decades building up and burnishing, quietly but steadily.

The time that Shintani-kun and I were spending was starting to grow in the same way. It wasn't a flashy kind of romance—we hadn't even slept together yet—and we were both a little serious, like schoolchildren, or characters in a Korean teledrama. But I felt like the town was showing me that I didn't have to hurry.

The old wooden beams, the glazed ceramic dishes, and the wrinkles on the reddened faces of the customers seemed to say: *Everywhere else in this country seems to tell you Go faster. So just while you're here, take your time; hesitate; lose your nerve; give up, sometimes. Everyone has troubles and weaknesses, and you can only try so hard. You'll be who you are. We're all of us different from one another.*

I felt like Shintani-kun's advice not to rush also applied to our relationship, and that reassured me, since I didn't want to rush anything just now.

The dilapidated bar was laden with half-eaten dishes and half-empty drinks. Even that unglamorous sight seemed only to underline my new confidence that things were okay as they were.

IT WASN'T LONG AFTER that that I discovered that Mom had a job.

One evening, I'd been able to take a short break, and went to a tea house to pass the time. There, I found Mom at work, in a traditional-style apron.

"Mom? What are you doing? Minding the shop?" I couldn't see Eri, the manager, anywhere, so I thought Mom had agreed to watch the shop for her.

"Nope, I work here. Since two days ago. I was always waiting for you to get home, and I used to take *sencha* lessons as a hobby before you were born, so I thought I could even manage to brew some tea in a pinch, with some training," Mom said, calmly.

"Oh, right, wow . . ." I was taken aback. Had Mom written up a resumé? Had an interview?

I took a seat and said, "May I have a *yuzu-kombu* tea, then, please."

"And what would you like to go with it?" Mom asked, bringing me the small tray holding samples of the sweet and savory accompaniments.

"Um, the pickled plum crackers, please," I said. It was just like playing make-believe with her as a child, I thought, and I felt embarrassed. But Mom was unperturbed, and went behind the bar and started calmly preparing the tea.

Then Eri-chan came back into the shop, and said, "Oh, Yocchan! Your mom's agreed to start helping me out," giving me her usual serene smile, which made me stop worrying about the complicated feelings I was having.

Eri-chan got back to work, moving briskly, and around me—regardless of my turmoil—the shop was filled with an air of peaceful calm. The atmosphere had been cultivated through the decades of the tea house's existence, a living thing that was continually being replenished. The teas stood orderly on the shelves, and the customers each spent their time in the space as they pleased. The sound of water boiling and the quiet music playing in the background melded until I heard them as a single sound.

I guess I have less to worry about if Mom's got a job, I thought. *It beats her being bored at home painting her nails, or walking aimlessly around the neighborhood, or sitting alone reading.* But standing inside the counter talking in a low voice with Eri-chan, Mom looked like the old Mom, from when she'd been herself, and my heart ached just a little in jealousy.

I'm the one who didn't want Mom to get better, I realized. I was shocked at my own immaturity. I was the one who wanted her to stay at home in my apartment, who wanted to keep my mother to myself. Now, standing in this shop, she was back in the wider world, among everyone else.

I sipped the tea Mom brought me, feeling chastened. It was sweet and good.

Of course . . . I realized, again. *Time's passing.*

I needed to get back on my feet again, too. I couldn't keep escaping into Dad's death. I wanted to stop feeling sorry for myself and how such a terrible thing had happened while I was still trying to get on my own feet. It had happened, and there was nothing to be done about that. There were plenty of people in the world who'd been through far worse. It had come as a huge shock to me, because it had been so far out of the normal flow of things until then, but it wasn't out of the realm of things that were possible in this world.

It consoled me to see Mom being moving around and smiling to people for the first time in a long time. I felt like something was coming back. Something like the shine of a time when the three of us were working hard to build our family. Something along with the plaintive cleanness to be found in the pain of loss.

For a moment, I thought it might be okay to forget about Dad like this, gradually, like I was leaving him behind. That going back over things and trying to figure out what happened, or trying to get closure, visiting graves and offering prayers, could all wait, maybe for decades. The sight of Mom getting on with her work was settling me into the present, into reality. The rest of the tea house—from the small flowers in a vase on the table, the steam rising from the kettle, the silver pot holding hot water for refills—all helped me see that I was here now, and there was no need to panic or be impatient.

But it wasn't to be. The other me inside me—the dark, damp, perseverating one—was still calling more things into my life.

THE WOMAN TURNED UP at Les Liens just before the end of lunch service one day.

She came through the door behind a swarthy man with dark features, who said, "We just want a cup of tea." She stood and stared at me from behind him.

"We close at three, is that all right?" I said.

"Yes, please," said the man. I couldn't place it, but he had a trace of a regional accent.

The woman, who I assumed was his wife, had pretty, round eyes, and a slightly melancholy expression. She had quite a strong build, and she gave the impression of a hard worker used to being on her feet. She had a guidebook to Tokyo, so I thought they were tourists.

The two of them ordered coffee, chatted quietly for a while, and then asked for a slice of apple pie to share.

After serving them the pie, I went to sweep the sidewalk outside, and then got back into the kitchen to prep for dinner, and wasn't keeping a very close eye on the couple. I heard a chair scrape and went back to the dining room, expecting them to want to pay. The woman counted out exact change and handed it to me. I thanked her, and I thought that would be the end of it.

Then she said, "My name is Nakanishi. I've come from Ibaraki."

Ugh, not Ibaraki, I thought.

"We're in Tokyo to attend a memorial for a relative, but there's something I wanted to talk to you about . . . about your father," she said. "Could you give me five minutes? My husband's waiting outside, as you can see, so I won't take any more of your time. I came here hoping to speak to you."

"I understand," I said, and nodded, feeling nervous, and went to get permission from Michiyo-san, who took one look at my expression and immediately said yes.

The woman started talking, still standing by the cash register.

"The man waiting outside is my second husband. My previous husband was nearly killed . . . by that woman," she said.

My vision went dark. In an instant, I saw what it meant to meet someone—it meant connecting with them, for good or for bad.

"In my case, their suicide pact failed, so it only destroyed our marriage. But that woman had been looking for a man to drag down with her for a long time. She was known for it locally. She worked at a hostess bar, and tried to get her clients to die with her.

It wasn't just her looks—there was something about her that well-bred men with a weakness found irresistible, and got sucked into. They were wrong to let themselves be, of course, but that woman bewitched them. My former husband lived with her for a while after we separated, but he fell ill and died a long time ago. I imagine she sucked the life out of him. There are people who will do that."

"I see . . ." I felt strangely touched to know that there was someone else who had gone through what Dad had.

I even thought, coolly, *It was Dad's fault for falling for it, then. How careless of him.*

But I also wondered what could have happened to make a woman turn out like that—like a kind of black hole. I was connected with someone whose world was so alien to mine, I couldn't even attempt to understand it, and not just by blood, but in more definite ways, too.

"So I'd like to visit your father's grave, if I may," the woman said.

"Oh, no, there's no need. I'll bear your kind wishes in mind when we hold the next memorial," I said. I was afraid that Mom might fly into a rage if I told her about this.

"It's hard for me to know that he died, you see . . . I feel that I'm partially responsible," the woman said. Her eyes were teary. "If you wouldn't mind, could you tell me where his ashes are buried? I'd just like to offer a prayer, and burn some incense. That's all. It would put my mind at rest."

"There's really no . . . I'm still very confused, there are so many things I'm not ready to think about yet. I can tell you where the cemetery is, if that's what you'd like. But please, leave my mother and me in peace," I said.

"I understand how you must feel. I just want to make a brief visit. It will help me. Although, if you're thinking of offering a service for him locally at any point, I know someone who would be able to help you, so please let me know."

The woman looked into my eyes, and I saw that hers were clear, but brimming with tears. There was nothing troubling in them. I could tell she meant what she was saying, and I got the impression that she was free of the problem now, and happy.

"If you're ever in Ibaraki, even if you're just passing through, please get in touch. I live in Kashima. I feel it was my former husband's fault, for living, that your father had to die. I keep thinking if my husband had taken that woman with him then, this would never have happened."

"No, it was my father's own fault," I said.

"I don't believe so. My husband involved himself with her in a halfhearted way, and the consequences of that went to your father. I'm so sorry. I still think about it, it's been on my mind ever since I read it in the paper, and I thought that visiting his grave was the only thing I could do, so I had to come here," she said.

I told her the name of the cemetery where Dad's grave was. The woman and the dark man took each other's arms, and walked off toward the station.

Dad—who was always seeing the best in everyone, who gave himself stomachaches from taking on other people's problems, who always had the air of being the one who'd draw the short straw. *That was what you did,* I thought, and missed him terribly.

I'd been over everything so many times in my head, but when I started thinking about Dad, I just couldn't let it go. Why, when nothing was going to bring him back, did I feel so strongly that I needed to do something for him?

It felt almost like being secretly in love with someone—wanting to help somehow, even if they didn't even notice, or never knew. The feeling of wanting to have someone's back, and longing to give them strength.

I WAS OVERCOME BY the desire to call Yamazaki-san, and gave in.

I called him from the Starbucks near the station on the east side, clutching my cell phone.

Why didn't I want to call Shintani-kun in this situation? I wondered briefly. The reason was that I was afraid he'd drop everything to go to Ibaraki with me, and want to help out with doing whatever needed to be done. I wasn't ready to close the distance between us so suddenly.

"*Moshi moshi,* hello?"

Yamazaki-san answered in the same voice he always did, and my agitation quieted immediately. I started to feel ashamed at having called him instead. The effect was immediate.

"It's Yoshie. Do you have time to talk now?" I asked.

"Yes, I do. But what's happened?" he said.

"Um, it's nothing serious, but I can't talk to Mom, and I wanted to tell someone, so I thought of you. A woman from Ibaraki came in to the bistro earlier, and told me her ex-husband had made a suicide pact with that woman, too. He survived, but died later of ill health, but she asked to organize a prayer service for him in the forest, and, well, I panicked, and told her the name of the cemetery, and I think maybe I shouldn't have done that. I wasn't really thinking straight. I feel like I've lost track of what I'm doing, what's right . . ." I said, and then regretted it instantly.

I was making a fool of myself. It sounded like I was coming on to him, feigning helplessness and acting like a child. But I had nowhere else to turn. Yamazaki-san's voice was the only thing that could get through to me. Sometimes you did things even if you knew they were unwise. I understood just how much Dad must have relied on him, before.

I wanted to see Yamazaki-san's face, and hear his voice— then I would feel safe. He would never make demands on me, and nor would he sacrifice anything for me, either. He had his own agenda and his own beliefs, and would never say anything that didn't align with them. I trusted him to do that.

"A prayer service . . . for your Dad? Why? It's nothing to do with her," Yamazaki-san said, sounding incredulous.

"She says she feels guilty," I said.

"I see, yes. I can see her point," he said. My mind was quieting, and I could hardly recall now why I'd been so panicked a few minutes ago about having given the woman the name of the cemetery.

"If you're thinking of going back there, would you like me to come with you? In case this woman turns out to be soliciting for a cult, or something. I'm assuming your mother would go, too? You might want a man along, in an isolated place like that. And I could drive," he said.

I was glad. When it came to Dad, I had allies. Shintani-kun was another. His death had led to new relationships—things had been born, too. I wasn't going to give up.

"I need to give it some more thought. May I call you again?

I don't want to tell my mother too much. She's finally starting to get back to her old self—she's just found a part-time job—and there aren't many people who were actually close friends with Dad," I said.

It had dawned on me while I was saying this that Shintani-kun was too decisive, too proactive for me to discuss this with. I was afraid that if I took this to someone who was used to thinking in terms of getting results, a chain of actions might be put into motion without my agreement, and beyond my control.

"Well, he was too timid, and serious, and too much of a pessimist to have a lot of friends!" Yamazaki-san laughed. I laughed too, carefree, like I used to be when Dad was still around.

Even this insignificant conversation was more than just an exchange of words. Feeling confident that what you wanted to say had been safely received, the ease of knowing that the other person wasn't putting themselves out, trusting them not to say anything they didn't mean—Yamazaki-san and I had given each other all of those things, too. Because we both shared our best memories of the time when Dad was here, we were trying not to destroy a single precious piece.

"I think you should treat it as a celebration of sorts," Yamazaki-san said. "I'd like to take part. I feel like doing something for him will be good for me, too. Every time I meet up with the rest of the band, we keep saying we should do a memorial show, a few years down the line. Whenever your mother feels ready to come, of course. So we can play all his songs without making anyone burst into tears. I bet he'll hear it, wherever he is up there.

"And, I know! If we're heading out to Ibaraki, we can stop by the Oarai aquarium on our way back. I'm an aquarium fan, too, same as Imo. We used to go visit them in downtime when we were on tour—Osaka, and Okinawa . . . and Ibaraki has hot springs, too. Let's do it," he said.

I knew he was making it sound like fun for my benefit, but his delight also sounded genuine enough that it raised my spirits. I was starting to picture how much lighter I'd feel, and how enjoyable it might be, if the three of us could visit that forest, offer up a prayer, and then go and do something fun on the way back.

"Thank you for the idea—I'll see what Mom says, too," I said.

THE LIGHTS IN THE Tsuyusaki Building looked even warmer in winter than they did at other times of the year.

It seemed like the light seeped into every nook and cranny of the dilapidated building, and out into the winter air. I'd loved that building, which Les Liens occupied part of, for a long time. The feeling of the shops lodging inside a space where people lived gave a softness to the whole street corner. The old windows and the loud, creaky stairs felt as though they belonged to a bank of nostalgic, shared experiences that everyone had known at some point.

The daily lives of the owners who lived upstairs, the cherry tree, the colorful shop signs—all of these cohered into a single impression that defined the atmosphere around the building. On gray, overcast days, I'd catch sight of its lights and feel warmth bloom in my chest. And in any season, I felt proud to work in the historic building.

That morning, when I arrived at the bistro, Michiyo-san looked downcast. Sitting at the bar, sorting through receipts with her eyes down, she was sending off an energy that was very different than usual.

"Has something happened? You seem a little low," I said.

"This place is going to be demolished. I have to close the shop at the end of the year," Michiyo-san said slowly.

"What??" I was so shocked, I said the first thing that came into my mind. "What's going to happen to the restaurant? And me?" I realized that I'd come to assume, again, that things would stay the same as they were today: tomorrow, the day after, next month, next year. I knew it wasn't true, but I never remembered that until things suddenly changed.

"No idea, I only heard today. I'd heard it was too run-down to restore, but it's finally happened," she said, quietly.

"I thought this building was some kind of protected cultural heritage. That it would be preserved," I said, nonsensically, not yet grasping the enormity of the situation. At the same time, I marveled at how I was already getting used to the idea. The moment I heard the news, there was a space in which I accepted it, which grew as time went on. That went for everything.

"I thought so too, but apparently they can't. It's not that Mr. and Mrs. Tsuyusaki don't want to, but there are complications with their landlord, who owns the plot. There's nothing to be done," Michiyo-san said.

"I see . . ." I nodded.

Michiyo-san looked at me, and said, "The thing is, I like this town, and I like our customers. This is where I want to work. So I'm going to take a few months off, go to France, and when I get back, maybe in six months, I'll open a new place. I won't find anywhere this cheap, because I agreed to rent knowing it was going to be taken down, so it'll probably end up being slightly smaller, but I've got some savings, and I'll make it work. So, Yocchan . . ."

"Yes." Nervous, I waited.

"I'd like it if you'd come work at my next place, too. I can't guarantee to pay you as much, but I'll do my best, and I can give you two months' pay while I'm on my break, as a thank-you."

"I'm so glad! Oh, not about the money, I mean," I said. "I'll gladly follow you to your next restaurant. I love your food, and Shimokitazawa. I can even help you look for a new premises, if you like."

"I appreciate it. Let's focus on seeing this place out in style, first." She smiled.

"Michiyo-san . . . When you go on your trip, will that be with someone, I mean a boyfriend, or friends, or . . . ?" I asked.

"Nope, I'll be solo. Not that I even have a man to bring. I haven't had the time. Well, I'll be seeing a girlfriend who lives in Paris when I get there, and on my way back. I'm thinking a month or two."

"If I may . . . could I come with you? I don't think I could afford to stay for two months, so maybe just for a few weeks. I'd like to see the direction you'll be taking next with your food. I can't speak French, so I'll probably only get in your way, but I'd be grateful if you'd consider it," I said, on the spur of the moment. For that instant, I'd forgotten all about Dad and been filled with a new strength.

"Sure. I was planning on staying with my friend in Paris for the first while, and then traveling around the north or the south of France for the rest. I need to go to Brittany, and I'd like to see Provence as well. Or wherever I can. We can travel around together. We can meet up in Paris, so give me a budget, and I'll find you a hotel. My friend's apartment is too bijou for us to both stay." She smiled. "Let's eat some good cheap food, and work on the menu for our next place."

"Thank you. I'd love that," I said. I wanted to think of this as something positive, not a forced retreat. Otherwise, I'd feel too bereft.

"I like this building a lot, and I was feeling depressed about having to leave," Michiyo-san said. "I thought you'd want to quit, too, but now I have something to look forward to. I'm glad to have you with me, Yocchan. Thanks.

"I loved this bar, and the little window. And the old toilet. We've only got a little longer, but let's take care of this old building, so it can leave this world happy. I'm sad we have to leave this place, but I feel privileged to have spent time in it. Almost like after all these years, the building chose me to spend its last moments with."

Michiyo-san was only saying commonplace things in an ordinary way, but her words felt to me like a breath of fresh air. It had been a while since I'd heard anyone talk about this kind of thing—the everyday love of someone truly committed to a specific place. That attitude seemed to be so on the decline everywhere that the occasional touch of it felt especially reassuring.

"I'd like to do that too," I said.

I was certain I wouldn't regret following her lead.

How lucky I was, I thought. If I'd found dishes hard work, or getting up early a chore, or being on my feet all day exhausting, or prep boring, I wouldn't have felt this way, and would have rushed to set up on my own, and made a bad shop. I felt like it had taken some emotional fortitude, almost like a kind of muscle I'd developed, to be able appreciate the gift that was Michiyo-san.

Since arriving in this town, I was becoming more and more honest, open, and grounded. At first, I'd come through like a tourist, but now, I could feel every one of my footsteps leaving a mark on the ground here, and sense how they added up over time.

Each day I walked this town, every step my feet inscribed, I was also building my inner landscape. They'd keep growing, in tandem, and a hint of my presence would linger even after I was gone . . . I was experiencing that form of love for the first time.

It was something I could never have learned in the town I'd grown up in. Back in Meguro, I hadn't ever had to stand on my own two feet. If I went back now, I would of course feel nostalgia, longing. But that would come with a burden of heaviness, and darkness, too.

When all this business with Dad was settled, I would probably be able to call that place my hometown. The day would come eventually.

But here, in Shimokitazawa, Mom and I were living our truth. Breathing like ourselves.

Couldn't we start over here, with Dad, all three of us? I thought.

It was too late for that.

I felt tears rising, and looked out the window. People were walking peacefully down Chazawa-Dori.

If the two of us as we were now—me, having taken it day by day, struggling through sweat and back pain and hangnails, earned someone's trust, and found myself a plan for the next little while; and Mom, having let go of the need to live up to the Madame lifestyle, and gone back to being her candid, jolly self— if only we could have lived with Dad in this town, we might have succeeded in building something lighter, and different.

Why did being alive have to mean that the body recovered, even when the soul couldn't?

No—that was the wonderful thing, of course. The body helped.

Right around now, Mom would be inside the soothing traditional-style space of the tea house, at work, moving her body in ways she hadn't known before, getting hungry, getting tired. As her body lived and metabolized, as its cells renewed themselves, she moved forward, step-by-step, leaving Dad behind.

Dad's absence in our lives now was so complete it almost felt cruel. In six months' time, I would be in a place I'd never been before, being stimulated by lots of new experiences, continuing my journey toward the flavors of the next phase of my life.

Of course, there were some things that didn't change—the familiar and nostalgic colors and smells, tastes, and places in our memories.

But we could no longer relive them as things that were real to our own bodies. I'd never smell Dad's back again—I could only recall how I once had.

How brutal life was! How fleshly, and mundane.

I was reeling, from having understood it for the first time.

What was lost would never return.

In its place, I now knew the smell of Chazawa-Dori in the rain.

I knew the energy and the particular thrill of walking though the buzz of young people on the main shopping street on the east side on a sunny day toward the station.

Six months ago, I hadn't even met Shintani-kun. He might have known of me, but I'd known nothing of him.

I'd been struggling so hard trying to forget Dad, trying to move forward; but my body, regardless of my effort, had already sneakily insinuated itself into the present. I could hardly fault Dad for having been carelessly drawn over to the other side. Our bodies forgot, left things behind, without our hearts meaning to. Then the things that were left behind curled up somewhere deep inside us, and hunkered down. Time didn't move at the same speed for them, so they always left a lump, something unresolved.

How do I let this go? I wondered.

I didn't feel enthused about seeking out the woman from Ibaraki again, and giving us more to share. A formal ceremony might have been the correct thing to do, but I just couldn't picture me and Mom kneeling there in that forsaken forest and praying. It seemed more realistic, and relevant, to think about us visiting Oarai aquarium. If Dad's spirit needed pacifying, well, this life would have to be enough. It was the truest prayer I had to offer.

Since what happened with Dad, we'd stopped wasting our lives, wasting time. We'd given up thinking about things as though we understood them, or even as though we could, and committed to living our days like a continuous length of thread we were each spinning.

ONE AFTERNOON, WHEN I was having thoughts like these, I met up with Shintani-kun in Shinjuku.

I was accompanying him to the Conran Shop, where he wanted to do some shopping—a fairly normal setup for a date. It felt strange, enough to make me realize I hadn't been on a real date in a long time. Standing there in my dress, I felt like I was a character in a play standing against the wrong backdrop.

I was on the first floor, watching Shintani-kun approach. As he walked across the shiny floor through the throng of people, the hem of his light coat flapping, I drifted into thought.

I was getting to love his face. There was absolutely nothing about him I didn't like. I admired the way his boldness and calmness showed themselves in his eyes, his mouth. The part of me who wanted to act my age gravitated toward him. If only we'd met at a better time, I thought, how captivated I might have been, and how much I might have suffered!

The way I saw him was strangely painful, like the way a married man might look at a girlfriend he loved to see— looking at someone who wasn't right for you, although they might have been, in a different time and place. You could call it the gift of perspective, and it was probably what had enabled things to be so easy between us, but I felt a little resentful, too. I tried to imagine if this was how someone might feel if they reconnected with their first love, once they were both middle-aged. They were still the same people, but to tell the truth, they would have preferred to meet each other in younger bodies, with fewer responsibilities and nothing to worry about.

Shintani-kun, unaware of my complicated feelings, spotted me through the crowd, smiled, and walked faster.

"I've been excited about replacing my sofa with a better one since I tripped and spilled coffee on it the other day, when the power went out," he said. "It was an old imitation leather one I brought from my folks' house."

"I don't think I've heard you mention your parents' place. Where was it? Near Shinjuku?"

"Um, a place called Nippori. My mom and dad got divorced when I was in college, and now my mom lives in Kobe, where her parents are. My dad stayed in the house, and he remarried, so they live there now."

"I see. My parents lived in Yanaka when I was young. That's close to Nippori, right?"

"What a coincidence! Do you remember it?" Shintani-kun's eyes shone.

"No, I was just a baby," I said, feeling bad for not remembering.

"Too bad. I love that area, it's so peaceful. There are so many temples, and everything's up a hill. Let's take a walk around there sometime," he said, with the air of someone telling you about his beloved hometown.

"I wonder if the apartment block we lived in is still standing. I'll ask Mom," I said.

I felt subdued. I'd assumed that Shintani-kun hadn't had any troubles in life, having simply taken over the family business, but of course, very few people got through life with no hardships at all. My family was in tatters, but in one sense, we hadn't divorced, or given up on being a family, which might mean we'd been happier than his.

We picked out a pretty sofa with thick blue fabric for Shintani-kun's apartment. Darker colors would be better for hiding stains, we'd agreed, seriously, like an old married couple.

"That ended up costing much less than I expected, so let me treat you to dinner," he said.

"Oh, no, I didn't even do anything, just tagged along," I said.

"Well, you always feed me well," he said.

"That's all Michiyo-san." I laughed.

"There's an excellent Korean restaurant near my place. Do you want to try it?" he said smiling, ever the food lover.

"Okay, since Mom's working all day today," I said.

"Your mom has a job? Where?" he said, surprised.

"The Japanese tea house opposite the flower shop. She serves tea, and takes care of the pet turtles," I said.

Shintani-kun laughed. "I'm going to go in there sometime, pretending I don't know a thing," he said. "Wow, so if I want to see the Imoto women, all I have to do is head to that street."

"Don't be so sure," I said. "We might be too fast for you. We don't have a lot of stuff, so we could make a pretty quick escape."

"But it still feels strange to me. I need something and pop out to 7-Eleven, with my purse. And when I walk down Chazawa-Dori, I get a weird feeling. A kind of loneliness, but also freedom, like I'm on vacation somewhere.

"A long time ago, when I was young, but after we'd moved to Meguro, Dad took me to the main street on the east side of Shimokitazawa Station. Just the two of us, by bus. It was so crowded, I asked him whether it was a festival, and he said, *No, it's always like this here on a Sunday*, and we held hands and walked down the street. The decorations were waving in the wind, and the way people's voices overlapped each other sounded just like music to my ears, and when we sat down for a cup of tea,

I still felt like I was looking at a festival in a foreign country. Dad bought some vinyl, and got me a little purse.

"It's only a small thing, from an ordinary day, but with the weather and the festival atmosphere, and Dad being in a good mood, and how I used that purse for a long time, it's turned into a really important memory to me.

"Sometimes now, I look up at the sky, and feel exactly the same as I did that day—as though I was out on a journey. I think it's because there are different people there all the time. But since I actually live there now, even if I'm walking around with my head in the clouds like that, I end up running into someone I know. We only say hello, or catch up for a minute, but it grounds me.

"The most important thing is, I have this sense that the feeling of holding Dad's hand that day is etched into the time within my body, but also into the town itself. That the memory will last forever, because the town was a witness."

"Wow," Shintani-kun said. "So even if you leave and come back again, they're still there. The marks you made will stay."

"Yes, I think they won't disappear, even if I lose my memory. Even if Dad's dead. I think places have that kind of power, as long as we love them. Even after someone dies, their feelings are marked there, like the lines on a CD."

Our home in Meguro had also been the place where I'd spent my adolescence, which had come with its own struggles.

The place was dense with memories: A phase when I hated Mom and her complete assumption that we were on good terms, so much that I could barely stand her touch, but never let on; the times I was sick with envy, in a grass-is-greener kind of way, of families whose dads came home at the same time every evening. The fact that I'd spent a lot of my time there feeling unequipped to deal with what I was going through and trying to tune it out probably contributed to me not being able to claim Meguro as my hometown, yet.

Of course, if Shintani-kun and I were to split up acrimoniously enough to no longer be on speaking terms, Shimokitazawa would look dull and gray, too. If Michiyo-san decided to open her new shop in Aoyama, I'd move over there. Everything flowed, everything changed.

One of the things you lost sight of when you lived in the city was the sense of how much power an individual had.

For example, even a major bookstore inside a large building would have its star staff members, who'd be missed if they moved to a different branch. But as Mom was saying, they'd immediately be replaced by someone new, and the shop would keep on running. People who lived in cities actually felt safer that way, I thought. That the world went on without them, that businesses wouldn't fold, that the town would keep functioning.

But it was human nature to be dissatisfied by that, too.

Recently—probably especially since losing Dad, and seeing his old band break up—I'd been thinking a lot about the power that one person could have. What it meant for someone to be irreplaceable, that things had to end if they left. For something to have to end that way, even if it had had a good run. And how that made you realize that you had to be a little greedy about making the most of what was now.

Being told, logically, that there was no time like the present didn't mean much, but when someone disappeared from a community, you suddenly cherished the days you'd had with them. People were only really capable of grasping things on that kind of scale, I thought. When I considered the destruction of the earth, I felt like I'd deal with it when I saw it happening, but when I thought of losing Shimokitazawa, I felt real fear. I guess that was just the way things worked.

If Miyuki-san left that small, bustling Thai restaurant, if her slender arms stopped shaking those sauté pans by the window, the taste of her cooking would be lost forever. If Tecchan, her husband, were to die suddenly in an accident, that would change the flavor, too, into something sad and dejected. When I passed by the colorful restaurant on a summer evening and smelled the spices, and heard the sounds of the kitchen, I got nostalgic for Thailand, even though I'd barely spent any time there. When the restaurant's yellow lights shone brighter as the darkness fell, they made me long for somewhere to go home to. Once I was inside, the smiles of the two of them as they greeted me transformed the melancholy of sundown into an equal amount of joy, as though through some kind of alchemy. And all it took for that magic to happen was for just two people to exist in this world and to find each other.

If Hacchan disappeared from the secondhand bookstore, we'd stop stopping by to see how he was doing when we passed the shop. The stacks of books and things that lay on the wooden floor, waiting to find their place, and the gallery area with its strange pictures made it feel like the place was his home, and drew lonely people inside to spend time with him.

If Eri-chan didn't put her heart into caring for them every day, the turtles in the tea house would probably die before long, just as the teapots and teacups would lose their shine, and look lifeless.

The same went for Les Liens. If Michiyo-san got discouraged, and started slacking off on her cooking, her famous barley salad would lose the lightness that came from her deft touch and start weeping moisture onto the plate, and the whole shop would grow stale and dingy and old.

If Chizuru-san, who ran Mom's favorite bar, were to leave, the town would become clouded by the unhappy sighs of her middle-aged clientele who were left with nowhere to go.

It seemed incredible that everything relied on just a handful of individuals in that way. Frankly, I would have preferred never to discover such an alarming thing.

This discovery also confronted me with my own responsibility. If I worked at the bistro for long enough, customers would start coming to the restaurant to see my smile. They'd start counting on me, almost like family, even though we weren't. They'd come looking, not just for Michiyo-san's food, but our work as a team in bringing it to them.

I felt dizzy at the enormity of it. I marveled at how people could pretend to be unaware of such an amazing fact.

Before going to the Korean restaurant, we decided to stop by Shintani-kun's apartment so he could lend me some CDs.

Which was to say, I'd signaled that I was prepared to take our relationship deeper.

We'd been seeing each other for a while now, and had become used to linking arms when we walked, or holding hands. I was almost surprised by how unremarkable it felt to be standing outside his door.

I wondered whether Shintani-kun would be nervous, too,

but he unlocked and opened the front door without hesitation, since it was his place, after all.

The first thing I saw was a small, wood-cased Tivoli radio speaker.

"I imagined you'd have a big hi-fi system," I said.

He laughed. "I don't really have the space," he said.

For a one-bed apartment, it was fairly spacious, but he lived more simply than I'd imagined. The laminate floor was clean and polished, and there was no hint of dust or mildew. The kitchen was obviously well used, and the pots and pans weren't brand-new, either, so I guessed he cooked for himself. The space felt comfortable and lived-in. A bottle palm with willowy leaves cast a strange silhouette against the light from the window.

When was the last time I'd been in a man's home, I wondered. What was this peculiar feeling it always gave me? The sense that this wasn't my own home, it belonged to someone whom I still felt some distance from, and it was an unfamiliar space. But I also trusted that I was wanted here, desired. It was a feeling I could never get used to.

"Tea? Coffee?" Shintani-kun said.

"Could I have coffee?" I said, and Shintani-kun got out a bag from Maldive, where we'd met, which made me feel even more at home. He operated the coffee machine in a smooth, practiced way.

"I like the way you do that. Can I headhunt you for the bistro?" I said.

Shintani-kun laughed. "I feel like that would mean you'd get paid less, and, knowing how efficiently you work, I doubt I'd have anything to do anyway, so, no thanks."

The town and the shop were a part of "us," something we shared. It comforted me enormously to realize that all the while I'd just been muddling through life, day by day, Shintani-kun had been there, too, and something had been growing between us, at its own pace.

I drank my coffee, feeling relaxed, like I was visiting an old girlfriend.

Then Shintani-kun put on some CDs he wanted me to hear. Some of them I thought I might get to like, but when he played his favorite—the band he had mentioned before, who had played at his venue—I was honestly unimpressed. Having been spoiled when it came to quality music, I found their sound flimsy and their performance immature. But Shintani-kun seemed invested in the idea that they were going to make it big, so I said nothing, and pretended to listen attentively.

Now that I came to think of it, I'd never been with a boy I could be totally honest with. Most of the time, the pattern would be that I'd hold back from mentioning something, thinking it wasn't really that important, and he'd insert his own assumptions into that space, interpreting things as he liked. I wasn't sure whether this was just because we were still young.

I spotted a framed photograph on a shelf of Shintani-kun as a boy, along with his parents. In the background was a festival float, food and toy stalls . . . some kind of happy celebration.

"Which festival was this?" I asked.

"Suwa Shrine," he said. "You turn down a street near the famous roast rice cake shop, and the shrine's on the hill, and it has a big festival every year. Mom and I would go all three days, and when Dad got home we'd all stay out until late. It must be one of the biggest festivals in the area. I still dream about the view looking over the town from the back of the shrine. I loved that festival even more than the one at Nezu Shrine, even though Nezu is more famous," he said.

"Your family was happy, then?" I said. *Like mine?* I thought. In the photo, Shintani-kun was flanked by his parents, wrapped in his dad's arms, and looked as treasured as a little prince. "We're both only children," I said.

"Yes, that probably explains why us leaving home kind of caused our parents to act like they'd left the family, too. I mean, what happened to your family was more than you all growing apart, but that was what it felt like for us. But everyone has their own problems. In my family it was so gradual, it felt kind of inevitable," he said.

"When I was a boy, we were really close. Living in the old *shitamachi*, entertainment was cheap, and we ate out a lot. Tonkatsu, Chinese food—nothing special. The main shopping street was down the hill from that shrine, and it was always full of people, and you could buy all kinds of food to take home. In the evening I'd walk down the hill holding hands with my mom. From the top of the stairs, the shopping street always looked like a festival," he said.

It was nice enough listening to his memories, his stories about the neighborhood he lived in as a child. It was agreeable— but that was all I felt. I didn't want him to add to the intensity of my life right now. *I don't think I'll ever meet your mom*, I thought despairingly. *We're probably going to sleep together now, but so what? What's it going to change?*

We were too young, and had too much ahead of us. There was no way we could stay this peaceful. I couldn't help but think that our tepid, pleasant relationship would get blown away by the first storm that blew across our path, like what had befallen each of our families.

So let's forget about families, and memories, and quit talking about things that take us forward like that, I thought, pessimistic. I didn't usually think that way, but everything felt too distant, like too much work, too wholesome.

But just then, the music by Shintani-kun's favorite band, which I'd dismissed earlier, suddenly started to sound beautiful, and the song's melody surrounded me, sweetly, softly. I felt touched by the sadness of youth and the anguish of doomed love they expressed, and I was startled. *It's true*, I thought, *They're talented, maybe they'll succeed.* I was impressed to realize that Shintani-kun understood music in his own way, albeit from a different angle than I did.

The momentary disillusionment I'd suffered about him melted away into the song's magnificence.

The singer's voice was idiosyncratic, but as gentle as could be, and seeped in through my ears even as I wallowed in cynical thoughts.

Perhaps he misinterpreted my silence: Shintani-kun picked that moment to suddenly put his arms around me and pull me to him.

Our first kiss was thus prefaced by incongruous feelings on my part, but even so, I was able to get a sense of Shintani-kun as a man, for the first time. I felt our bodies respond to each other. Whatever else was going on, we were after all dating, and I was brought back to the realization that desire was alive—that while my heart might be half dead, my body hungered unashamedly for the opposite sex.

After the kiss, Shintani-kun kept hold of me without saying anything. I heard his heart beating in his chest. *There's someone here,* I thought, *someone definitely here.* Then in a flash, I recalled the bodies. *It's no good,* I'd thought—*they're definitely dead.*

I can't do this, I thought despairingly. *I'm not ready for love.* I was on the verge of tears.

"Let's stop here for today. I think it's too soon for you," Shintani-kun said.

"When you put it that way, it makes me want to prove you wrong," I said, and smiled as I looked up at him, but my tears started to fall, in a pathetic and not at all attractive way, and I think my expression must have looked pretty bizarre, too.

"I'm not particularly interested in waiting. I'm a man, after all. But there's no rush. The town or the shop won't run away, and you're not going to disappear," he said, with kind eyes.

"Not a very lustful person?" I said.

"No, I'm a beast. I'm told I'm hard to keep up with, actually." He smiled. It was a grown man's smile. I couldn't tell whether he was serious.

"Come stay the night soon," he said, hugging me again. The palm of his hand pressed against my back suggestively, but I didn't mind.

"Okay," I said. "I'm fine—it's not like I was raped, or anything."

"No, I think what happened to you and your mom was even worse. I think you'd be justified in holding a grudge," he said calmly. I was grateful for his understanding.

"I'm angry enough at that woman already. I've had a peaceful life, and I've never hated anyone like this before. When I think about her, my mind goes dark," I said.

"I suspect you'd be justified in giving her even more of the blame," Shintani-kun said. "I think you're too generous."

I wondered whether that was true.

Of course, there were times when I was overcome by hatred for her, but I'd reached a place where I could take a step back and acknowledge that she must have been through a lot, too. And in any affair, responsibility lay with both the people involved. Dad wasn't an innocent victim. Plus, I'd never understand the reasons that had driven her to do it. My only guess was that not succeeding the first time might have given her a taste for it, but I had no intention of trying to look further into it. The brutal will to life that permeated my body throbbed in anger, seeming to say it would rather die than have sympathy for such a thing.

SITTING AT A LOW table in a tatami-matted section of the Korean restaurant near Shintani-kun's apartment, feasting on *jjigae*, barbecue salted tongue, and a selection of kimchi, and feeling relaxed, I brought up what was on my mind.

When we ate out, we always ended up with me picking at small dishes while Shintani-kun made short work of everything else. I'd be full at that stage, but he was only getting started. If we were ever to live together, I wondered, was he going to end up obese somewhere down the line? But seeing as we'd only kissed once, the thought had no immediate connection to reality. I still wasn't even sure whether or not I was in love—that was how easily we'd ended up here.

"Hey, Shintani-kun?" I said.

"What's up? Ready to move on to the *galbi*?" he said deadpan, looking at the menu, and I nearly laughed. I was pretty sure this was good breeding speaking, rather than a sign of a one-track mind.

"Earlier, you said something like I was nowhere near ready for a relationship. And, I was wondering whether that meant you were breaking up with me? Or even that we'd never been going out in the first place?"

"Wow, I think I would have felt pretty offended if anyone else had asked me that. But coming from you, I don't mind at all. I wonder why that is," he said.

"How should I know?"

"Yes, I don't know," he said, not joking. "That's not how I meant it. I just thought it didn't feel right. Wait, not like that— not that I wanted to split up." He turned pink in embarrassment, which was endearing. "I just suddenly got this feeling that if we slept together straight away, you'd end up hating me."

"I doubt that would happen," I said. "I don't think I'll ever hate you, even if we have to break up. But that's just because right now, I don't have very strong feelings like about anything."

"In that case, spend the night at my place next time. Because there's no way I could stay at yours." He smiled.

I marveled at the frankness with which he could talk about something this awkward, and realized he'd probably always had women in his life, and knew how to treat them. He was used to all of this. Why was he with someone as inexperienced as me? I wondered, and gazed at him.

The restaurant was full of families, and was run by one, too. The mother and the daughter-in-law in the kitchen, and the father and the eldest son at the front of house, called out orders to each other in loud but genial voices. The whole shop was like a big house, warm on the dark street.

Cocooned in its atmosphere, I'd temporarily forgotten my past troubles.

I had a boyfriend of sorts, and was getting along with Mom, and had some prospects at work—*I guess I might be moving toward some kind of relative happiness*, I thought vaguely. The feeling seemed to have been drawn up through me by the appetizing smell of grilling meat, the echo of ordinary conversations around us, and the peculiar freedom of a time of day when we forgot our daily worries and frustrations.

"Let's get some lamb on the grill," Shintani-kun said, carefree. "The lamb here is better quality than most you can get."

"Leave it to me," I said, and smiled. "I've been watching how Michiyo-san does it, to steal her secrets."

We ordered some excellent lamb, and waited for it to arrive, and grilled our hearts out, and devoured it with rapt attention.

My soul was lapping up the happiness that suffused the whole experience. For the first time in a long, long while, I felt joy springing from somewhere inside me. I felt thankful. *Thank you, Shintani-kun, for finding me—Even when I thought I wanted to be left alone, and invisible.*

MOM WAS CHANGING, TOO.

Since getting a customer service job, she seemed to have suddenly started standing taller. One night, I saw her with a face mask on for the first time in months. And it was no ordinary face mask, but an expensive, luxury hydrating mask from Guerlain, which she'd used often in Meguro.

"Wow, nice, Mom. The look takes me back. Did you buy it?" I said.

"Oh no, I retrieved them from Meguro. The expiry date was coming up, so I had to hustle," she said, easily.

So she was able to do that kind of thing now, I thought.

"You know, I've finally settled into this life enough to think about caring for my complexion. I may act like a student, but my skin's middle-aged," Mom said, and laughed.

"It's a good sign," I said.

"Yesterday I even splurged and went to the beauty salon. A upmarket, Madame-type place down the road, on the third floor above Tomod's."

"Wow, Mom, just like old times."

"I went for the Miracle Face Shrinking Machine. Don't you think my face looks a little smaller?" she said, proudly.

"Now that you mention it, your jawline looks trimmer, maybe," I said. It was true that she looked cared for, somehow.

"Right?" she smiled. "Being frugal is well and good, but I think it's important to do this kind of thing, maybe, oh, once every six months or so."

"It suits you," I said. "And it's good you have a job now, too."

"They're all good people at the tea house," Mom said, "and when we're busy, the customers don't mind waiting. Of course I don't get along with all of them, but Eri's always so steady, I can stay calm and be professional. All the other part-timers have been there long term, and the owner's a great person, too."

Mom never talked about Dad, but she wasn't over him. I knew that. But I was still surprised by the strength she was showing in rising up and moving forward. While I was crying over things, or generally feeling down, I felt she was using the same time in a more decisive way. I wondered whether that was the difference between having lost a father and lost a husband.

ONE EVENING, A LITTLE while after that, when I happened to be off work and was home in my apartment, Mom came home and suddenly said she wanted to go back to Meguro to fetch the beauty contraption that generated "misted steam" and so we went back to the condo together for the first time in a really long time.

Seeing the place empty was tough, as I'd expected.

Even without bringing Dad into it, as soon as we unlocked the door and came into contact with its silent emptiness, I felt like I was diving down deep into a nightmare. Once past the entry, the house smelled the way it always had, and I recognized a shadow of a time when the place had been alive. But everything had stopped now.

Mom went in briskly, opening windows and switching on lights.

I went to what had been my room, and gathered a few cookbooks and novels. Then I got out some other books and summer clothes I'd accumulated while I was in Shimokitazawa, and stored them away in the bookcase and the wardrobe.

The whole time, I felt like something was chasing me.

I looked over to the piano repeatedly, hoping Dad's ghost would visit, but he didn't. There wasn't even a hint of a presence. Everything was quiet and lifeless.

Had I really once lived here for so long? My fingers and my feet and my eyes all remembered the details of this condo, and I still knew its smells, the height of its doorknobs, how to rush down the hall without colliding with things, how to use the bathroom without switching on a light—all these stood out in my memory in sharp contrast, so familiar that I felt nauseous, but this space no longer belonged to me. The layers upon layers of accumulated memories had hardened into forms that stopped me from breathing in the present. When I looked at something, I saw it through a filter of hundreds of memories, which made everything darker, more layered, more intense. *It's like being inside a coffin*, I thought. I understood all too well why Mom had felt stifled here on her own and had needed to move in with me.

Mom was standing in the doorway to my room, holding a handbag full of cosmetics.

"Hey, Yocchan? I was thinking of suggesting we go for some French food around here, like we used to, but I'm suffocating a little from all the memories in this place. I didn't feel it when I dropped in alone, during the day, but with you here too I guess I let my guard down a little, and I'm feeling even sadder and more miserable," she said.

I nodded, relieved.

"Do you want to head home and get curry instead?" Mom said.

"Great idea! Was it open today?" I smiled. Our favorite curry place was a well-known restaurant with a rustic, wood-panelled interior like a cabin in the woods, five minutes' walk from our apartment.

"Yeah, I saw the sign was up, earlier. What will you have?" Mom said. "I'm going to go for the mushroom curry, today."

"I think I'll order the vegetable, extra spicy. A large portion," I said, giving it serious thought. Somehow, my mood lightened.

"Why is that curry so good, I wonder?" Mom said. "I always finish all the rice, too. There's so much sauce it almost spills off the plate, the abundance of it alone makes me feel rich and happy. Plus, you can really taste the gentle sweetness of all the vegetables that go into the sauce—no wonder the shop's named after an eggplant!" she said, smiling. How long had it been since I'd seen her smile properly here, I wondered, touched. Her smile against the backdrop of the condo's white walls felt like home.

"Okay, I'll be over there doing some cleaning, so tell me when you're done here," she said.

"Will do," I said.

It was an ordinary conversation, but it was a decisive moment for both of us—a sudden and unexpected desire to go home to Shimokitazawa, and turn down that particular alley, which led to that specific restaurant. To feel the recognition and relief at seeing the signboard standing out on the main street; to push open the heavy wooden door and enter the small, tranquil shop, which felt like the home of a good friend, and see the faces of the awkward and sincere waitstaff and the quiet husband and wife team who made such hearty curry, and feel safe.

Mom and I were probably each surprised at feeling this way, and also at finding out that the other felt exactly the same. Especially when we'd each held back, thinking the other might prefer to go somewhere in Meguro—somewhere from before.

Having invoked the neighborhood we lived now, I had the distinct sensation of time coming back under our control. The air in the condo, which had been heavy, suddenly lightened. I think that was the moment we resolved to leave that house. We had no more regrets. We were both clear that there was nothing left to do there.

As we were leaving, scuttling away with our bags, I was putting my shoes on in the entry.

"You probably won't like this idea," Mom said, as though something had just occurred to her.

I nodded. Somehow, I knew—I'd been thinking the same thing. "The photo of Dad? I don't mind. Let's take it."

"How did you know?" Mom said, surprised.

"I thought we should, too," I said.

Mom nodded and went inside.

She came back carrying the framed photo of Dad that had stood by his amp.

"We'll give him flowers every day, over there. I refuse to be defeated," Mom said.

"Yes, let's do that," I said.

I already had a photograph of the three of us above the TV in my apartment. But Dad's photo—the large, formal portrait that had stood at his funeral—was coming to our apartment for the first time.

"And I support you in refusing to lose. Although in some ways, we've already lost a lot, already. I might even say irretrievably," I said.

"How are you even managing to joke about this?" Mom said, laughing pretty hard. She closed the door behind us, and turned the key in the lock as we left what had once been home, but probably never would be again. Of course I knew we'd be back again for one thing or another, but I felt like when I looked back afterward, I'd know that this was when we'd said good-bye.

AFTER A DELICIOUS CURRY, we stopped by the small flower shop around the corner and bought a bouquet from the vivacious woman who worked there, who handed it to us with a smile, and went home and put it in a vintage milk bottle I'd found in an antiques store on Chazawa-Dori, and put it next to Dad's photo. Then I poured some essential oil into the oil burner, and lit the tealight. Its small flame cast a wavering light on the wall, and the calming smell of lavender filled the room.

Seeing Dad's photo surrounded by things that were so definitely of this neighborhood, I felt that Dad now lived in Shimokitazawa, too.

Something had come to an end, I thought, been settled somehow.

"Hey, Mom? I'm not saying right away, but the condo . . . do you want to sell it? Let it out?" I said.

"I'm leaning toward letting it," Mom said. "My friend who lives in San Francisco is coming back in about a year, and I might sell or let it to her and her husband when they do. She knows the circumstances, and she offered to rent it furnished, and for a generous rate, if I wanted. They're well-off, and she said since they wanted to live in Meguro anyway, it was the least she could do . . . So I guess I'll have to get rid of some things, gradually, and maybe look for a different apartment here, so I can move out of your place? I can't really take action yet, but that's what I'm thinking," Mom said.

"That sounds like a good plan," I said. "Dad won't be lonely, then, either."

"Don't worry about that, we moved him today. I'm leaving aside the unforgivable parts for the moment, but the main strand of his soul is here now, where it belongs," Mom said.

In the face of this assertion from Mom, his wife, I started to feel like it could be true.

THAT NIGHT, I DREAMED about the phone again.

The house in Meguro had been totally emptied.

There were no memories there, aside from the marks on the wall. Even the piano was gone. A square of light shone onto the floor from the window.

I was standing there in shock. *Has the move already happened?* I thought vaguely. *That was quick. But wait, where do I live now? Where are my things? Am I still looking for somewhere to go?*

My phone rang. I took it out of my bag and answered.

"*Moshi moshi?* Hello?" I said.

"*Moshi moshi*," said Dad.

"It's okay, your photo's in Shimokitazawa already," I said. Tears were rolling down my cheeks. "Dad, Dad, you don't hate us, do you?" I said. He didn't reply.

I cried and cried, and couldn't stay on my feet any longer, and fell to my knees on the living room floor where I had so often lain as a child. Soon it would be covered with new carpet and strange furniture.

"I want to see you, Dad. Why do we have to talk on the phone?" I said.

The other me was pointing out that I had more important things to tell him. But in dreams we were always exposed, foolish versions of ourselves. On the other end of the line, I felt the usual quiet presence of Dad, who didn't hate us at all.

Oh, I thought. *He wanted to call. When he died—that was the thing he most wanted to do.* I was sure of it.

I WOKE IN THE middle of the night, and sat up suddenly in bed.

The smell of lavender oil was still in the air, and the candle was still burning. Dad's photo was in the room. He was smiling. He might already have been with that woman when the picture was taken, but he had still been alive and with us.

This wonderful smell and the offering of flowers must have given him a route into my dream, I thought nonsensically, still half asleep. I figured Dad was all right, now. I didn't know why, but the timing had been crucial. It couldn't have happened on any other day.

When I looked to my side, Mom was sleeping soundly. Some day, Mom and I would leave this world, too. But for now, she was here, and fast asleep, traveling through the dream world with her mouth half open. Here was someone I loved, who was still definitely here.

Relieved, I lay myself back down. Still half in a dream, I felt around briefly for my phone, which I thought must be close by, but I quickly fell into a deep sleep.

A feeling was enveloping me, a sense of relief that some of what I feared had finally gone. My apartment was full of a soft warmth, both inside my feather comforter and out.

I realized that the prospect of Dad wandering around unable to move on hadn't been the only thing I'd been afraid of. I'd actually been more anxious about the possibility that Mom had abandoned his memory and was moving forward without him.

IT WAS A FEW weeks later that the customer from Ibaraki came to the bistro again, alone.

We were at the peak of lunch service, and I had to make an effort to hide my annoyance.

Why did she have to come and remind me about things when I was just starting to feel some peace, and when I'd finally stopped dreaming about Dad? I would have been happy to forget that the whole prefecture of Ibaraki even existed.

"I'm sorry, I know it must be difficult for you to see me," the woman said, and ordered her food apologetically.

Even though it was difficult, I decided there was a limit to how aggrieved I could feel given that she was thinking of Dad and had come to the restaurant especially, even if she was in town for other reasons. I served her her food with a welcoming smile. The woman had a pleasant way of eating. She looked like she was really enjoying the taste of the food, and not as though she was eating it because she felt she had to in order to see me.

You could always read a person's state of mind in the way they ate a meal. No act or mask or correct table manners could fool the eyes of someone who watched people eat day in, day out, like I did.

Plus, I thought, it wasn't beyond the bounds of possibility that her going to the cemetery had somehow contributed to Mom and me feeling easier about things recently. Things in the world could be connected in ways I didn't necessarily understand.

I took the plunge and spoke to her as I served her coffee. "Thank you for visiting my father's grave when you were in town last time," I said. "My mother and I haven't been able to go as often as we'd like, and we're very grateful."

The woman's nervous expression released, and she smiled in relief.

I realized that she'd expected me to not want to talk to her. I'd been dreading seeing her again, myself, but when I looked into her eyes, the sincerity and goodwill there undid my defenses.

"I struggled after it happened to me, and I really felt that I ought to come back and see you," she said. "I'm sorry to have reminded you of things again. This is something I was given by the person I mentioned." She reached into her backpack and took out a small cloth pouch. Inside it was another, pretty pouch, neatly embroidered.

"What is it? Salt?" I said, taking a stab in the dark. I didn't know much about this kind of thing.

The woman nodded. *How had I known?* I wondered.

"Yes, it's salt. This person is one of the most psychically sensitive of anyone I know, and knew the background to it already, from when I'd asked for advice before. So I asked for something to help you. It might not do much, but you can take it with you when you visit his grave, or the place he died," she said, smiling.

That would be never, I thought, but I kept my mouth shut.

This woman had been through a great deal—having her husband stolen and nearly murdered, a divorce, and then his death. No matter whether or not she'd managed to find happiness after that, I was honestly in awe of how she was able to be so kind that it was verging on prying to someone she'd never even met.

If I were her, I'd have been afraid of getting chased away with salt myself.

"The reason I'm doing all this," said the woman, as though she'd sensed what I was thinking, "is because I feel that I understand—as much as anyone can—what you and your mother must be going through, more than anyone else in the world, as though we're connected somewhere deep underground. How you don't want to hate anyone, but you do. You don't want to blame anyone, but you do. You don't want to dwell on it, but you can't help getting bogged down."

This was all true for me, so I nodded. "I've never spoken to anyone who, um, knows about things that can't be seen, I guess. Did they say anything?"

The woman looked down, and then seemed to make a decision, and looked at me again.

"I was told—*She is the kind of woman who brings out a longing for death in men, the more they sleep with her.*"

I felt like something had stabbed me in the chest.

Every time I thought about it, Dad felt further and further away.

"My friend also said that woman was only around to find someone to die with, that she was already no longer part of this world. That there was no need to pity her, but no reason to despise her, either. That it was her problem alone. But it's difficult to feel that much acceptance about it, isn't it?" she said, with a slightly unusual intonation. I suddenly wondered whether that dead woman had spoken like this, too, and shivered.

"But those of us who are left go on living," she said.

Another table called for me, and I had to go.

I let her give me the pretty cloth pouch with the salt in it.

"Thank you. I'll keep it safe. And when I'm able to visit the place where my father died, I'll scatter it there," I said.

She drank her coffee slowly, and left with a smile—an unremarkably dressed, middle-aged woman with a rounded back and sturdy calves.

Someone I'd probably never see again, but to whom I was irrevocably connected for life.

Was that what it meant to be alive?

It felt almost like magic.

I WAS A FIRM believer in the idea that coincidences always came along at the right time. I felt there was some kind of reason for the way things happened as they did, like bubbles from my subconscious mind rising to the surface.

Since that day, the distance between me and Shintani-kun had grown much closer. Maybe we felt safer with each other, having voiced things that had been on our minds. I was feeling guilty for having misinterpreted Shintani-kun's reserve, and perhaps underestimated him a little. He was a lot more mature than I'd assumed, and genuinely seemed to have my interests at heart.

To be honest, somewhere deep down, I'd been rebelling against the suspicion that Shintani-kun had been drawn to me out of pity, as the poor girl who'd lost her father. I was gradually coming to see it wasn't true; that he understood more about me than that, and was attracted to all of me.

Thus the disdain I'd had for him had faded.

I still hadn't stayed the night at his place, nor did we ever kiss or grope each other impulsively by the side of the road or in elevators like high schoolers. But whether we were standing or sitting, we found ourselves more often casually holding hands, or just sticking close to each other.

One night after I'd finished work, as we left the bistro together, I was thinking how he wouldn't be coming in just before closing to sit at the bar, like he always did, for much longer.

At Les Liens we were slowly winding down, preparing for the end.

One day, Michiyo-san and I were going through and tidying shelves, and I overheard her mutter, "I guess we won't be serving the summer shave ices here again."

I felt the loss, too. I could still vividly recall the life-giving freshness of the barley salad, and the coldness of the shave ice, especially as they stood out against the backdrop of that rock-bottom summer.

As we cleaned up, Michiyo-san and I told each other that this was only a temporary pause, a waypoint, a new start. That while everything came to an end sometime, our partnership would continue, and there would be a new shop soon. That this was no time for grieving.

When we were done, Michiyo-san locked the door behind us and said, "I know we haven't left yet, but that felt like good-bye."

Although I knew the building was being demolished, I'd taken to putting even more heart into cleaning it. I wanted to scrub the floor so it glowed even warmer, to wash the windows so they let in even more light. It was like how I might feel about someone I looked up to. Each time I cleaned, I did it as though it were my one chance to do it right.

I almost wished I could feel this way about Dad. Most of the time, when I thought about him, I felt so resentful that he was gone that I gave in to disappointment and despair.

SHINTANI-KUN WAS WAITING FOR me at Chizuru-san's bar. He'd been wanting to try out an oatmeal stout that was on their menu called Shakespeare Stout. When I went down the stairs to the basement, through the seventies rock playing at high volume, I was greeted by the sight of him sitting at a table opposite Mom.

The bar was a unique space that gave the impression of being entirely covered in a mosaic of handblown glass, like something made by a drunken Gaudí. A giant lizard looked down from the ceiling. The décor was indescribable, reminiscent of Azteca or Spain, and the floor was full of tables made of slabs of wood with their bumps and hollows intact. The music was always loud, but it was a friendly bar with a cozy atmosphere.

That night, though, I wasn't appreciating the décor, or looking around at the other customers. I was riveted to the sight of the two familiar people sitting opposite one another.

It's not that strange, I told myself, trying to seem calm. *Mom comes here a lot, it's not that much of a coincidence.* I put on a smile and approached their table.

"Hi, Yocchan," Mom said. "Shintani-kun's really nice."

"What are you two doing drinking together like old friends?" I said. My legs were swollen from being on my feet all day, and I sounded almost petulant. I felt disappointed by how immature I was being. The worst surprise, though, was that my first feeling on seeing them together wasn't unqualified happiness. Truthfully, my gut reaction had been a kind of wariness, even dread.

"Sorry, we ran into each other, and got chatting," Shintani-kun said, looking genuinely apologetic.

"It's okay, I realize these things happen," I said, and laughed. A waitress came by, so I took a seat beside Mom, asked for the Red Fox Ale and some snow peas as I often did, and took off my coat.

I sometimes came here alone since it was open late, or with Mom when we were feeling peckish, so really, it was no big deal.

"Shintani-kun, I'm so glad we got to talk," Mom said. She drained her mixed drink, and said, "I'll see you back at home. I don't want to crash your date."

You're cool, Mom, I thought, but I said, "It's okay, let's walk home together."

"No thank you, you young people carry on. There's something I've been meaning to watch on TV, as well. I meant to tell you—I got Hacchan from the bookstore to help me move the big TV from Meguro," she said.

"Into that poky apartment?" I said. "What did you do with the old one?"

"I left it at the condo," she said.

"I can't believe it," I said. "That was left to me by a friend."

"But my eyesight's not as good as it used to be, I could never see anything on that poky screen. Plus it was so chunky and old-fashioned. Anyway, wait till you get home. Because the room's so small, everything looks really dramatic on it—it's like being in a movie theater," she said, smiling. "While I'm confessing, I should tell you I brought the smaller stereo, too."

"Wait, how much space do you think we have? Is there enough room left to lay out our futons?" I said, but inside I was secretly pleased. Mom was making an effort to enjoy her life as it was now. She was trying to integrate the past by bringing parts of her old home into the new one.

"I'll get the apartment warmed up for you. On the other hand, don't feel you have to come home, if you don't want to," she said.

"Hey!" I said, but she ignored me and paid our bill, and practically skipped up the stairs as she left.

"It was bound to happen sooner or later, I guess, since we go to all the same places," I said. I finally felt relaxed enough to start on my beer.

"Your mom's sweet," Shintani-kun said.

"So embarrassing," I said. "Drunk in the middle of the night. I'm sure she's going to get back and find she has nowhere to sleep, with the big TV and stereo in the room." I laughed.

"Oh, I nearly forgot. I'm kind of glad she's gone, actually, because of this," he said, and took a small bundle wrapped in cloth out of his bag.

I know this, I thought. *This happened recently.*

"I don't think I could have told your mom," he said.

"What is it?" I said.

He opened the bundle, revealing what looked like slips of paper with writing on them.

"Not again," I said, without really meaning to.

"What do you mean, again?" Shintani-kun asked, so I told him how the customer from Ibaraki had given me the bag of salt. He nodded thoughtfully.

After a pause, he said, "I mentioned before that someone had killed themselves, at the venue? And we had the space cleansed by someone from the local shrine. Since you said you might go to Ibaraki sometime, I went to the shrine and got these talismans. I thought they could help, even if you just took them with you."

"You, too?" I said in surprise.

"I'm not trying to tell you what to do," he said. "I just thought you might feel better if you had them. Sorry, I know it's none of my business, and it's not like you asked for my help. I'm not really sure why I even got them."

He sounded a lot like the woman had, which spooked me a little.

"I'm sorry I said that," I said. "And thank you."

Shintani-kun blushed, looking embarrassed.

I was getting fonder and fonder of him.

I didn't know what was holding me back anymore.

The ale was as bitter as sinking down into the pit of night. Like a child, I longed to forget where I was and what I'd done, and just go back to his place with him. The stuff with Dad still left lumps in my throat, like the pinbones of a fish, but Mom's changes were reflecting in me and I was slowly changing inside, too.

Shintani-kun and I could carry on like this, and grow closer, and commit to each other, and then time would pass, and all kinds of things could happen—we'd fight and make up, I'd go to France, and come back, and go back to work, and we'd pass the days, maybe move in together, or get married, have children . . . but none of this was certain. I could get hit by a car the moment I left the bar tonight and die, or meet someone in Paris and have an epic romance and never come back here again. Shintani-kun might go to work tomorrow night and get approached by someone so incredibly beautiful that he'd come to me and apologize and say he wanted to break up. So maybe it was better to go for things so I didn't regret it later. I was sure that was true.

Even so, there was something murky and inexplicable inside me that said that getting in deeper now would be too easy. It had something to do with Dad, and I was worried that if I moved forward without understanding it, I might end up pretending I'd never noticed it at all.

If you carry things forward as they were now, the murkiness seemed to say, *standing everything up straight and proud in the sunlight, you'll have a respectable kind of life, but any dark things will have to be hidden, pushed back down into the depths. And that's where things start to go awry.*

And when those little niggles accumulate and blacken deep inside, I thought, *they'll be a lesser version of what killed Dad.*

But I was tired of thinking about all this.

Part of me wanted to say it was too much trouble, to give into my desire to lean into him right then and there and lay myself against him and close my eyes. But there was still a thin film separating the normal me who would do these things from the me inside.

My instinct was telling me that if I took any action while this barrier existed, I would end up paying for it later. I didn't quite understand it, but I knew it was true. I wasn't being cautious, or overthinking it. I just couldn't help being aware of the barrier's existence.

Maybe I want to stay like this for now, I thought. *I think it's still safe. I don't want to imagine losing Shintani-kun, and he's not about to leave. I hope that's true, please let him wait,* I thought, lightly stroking the surface of the paper talismans he'd given me.

But I had no idea what I wanted him to wait for.

WHEN I GOT BACK to the apartment, the imposing flat-screen TV was standing on the shabby tatami mat floor, illuminating Mom's face like she was in a movie theater.

"I'm home," I said. "That TV has some presence."

"Oh, you came back," she said, sounding disappointed.

"Can't I come home to my own apartment?" I said.

"No, I'm glad. I wanted you to see how luxurious it looks now," she said, gleefully.

I started brewing some herbal tea.

"Your boyfriend's nice," Mom said.

"Yeah, he's smart, and he has good taste in music, even though it's different from mine, and he's got good manners, and can be endearingly naïve, and he's just a really good person. Um, so did he mention he runs that venue in Shinjuku?" I said.

"Yeah, he told me. It takes me back," Mom said. "I never really liked the way it smelled, or how loud it was, or the gin and tonics that were always way too strong and came in flimsy cups. I used to resent Dad for enjoying himself on stage like a young man while demanding his wife be the put-together Madame. Knowing what I do now, I'd be there dressed just like this, dancing my ass off and having fun. I was young, too, I guess. Young and serious. I probably felt like I needed to act responsible to make up for Dad being in a frivolous-seeming line of work."

I nodded. Then I said, "By the way, Mom, what are you watching?" I'd been wondering for a while. I felt like I might have seen the movie, once, but if I had, it had been so long ago, I'd completely forgotten the story. The actors playing the man and the woman were Yusaku Matsuda and Hiroko Yakushimaru.

"It's *Detective Story*. I walked past the jazz bar, Lady Jane, where Yusaku Matsuda used to be a regular, and suddenly felt like seeing his face again, so I bought it and put it on. What a masterpiece. And such good acting from both of them. I love this movie, I really do. Why on earth didn't I move here while Yusaku Matsuda was still alive? Then I might have bumped into him on the street at night, or something. I don't know what I might have done to him then," Mom said.

"I remember now, I saw this at the theater when I was small, with Dad," I said. "I was too young to understand any of it, though."

"That's right, Dad was a Yusaku Matsuda fan. I think he wished he could be more like him," Mom said matter-of-factly, like she used to do when Dad was alive.

There was a clue here, too, I thought, in the way the movie proceeded steadily forward through time, conserving all the interior heat it generated, and carrying it all toward a single point—the kiss in the final scene.

It was only when Michiyo-san came down with the flu that I understood quite how far I was from being fully fledged.

"I feel feverish. You'd better not come too near," she said. "In case it gets bad, let's streamline the lunch menu to just the couscous and the curry, and get them prepped."

Without saying much more, but clearly suffering, she started preparing the stews. I helped as much as I could, but when I saw what a hard time she was having, I couldn't help but feel I wasn't helping much.

"If we can get hold of Moriyama-san, we can definitely stay open tomorrow," I said.

"You're right," Michiyo-san said, "but let's worry about tomorrow when it comes."

Michiyo-san left everything prepped and went home, and I had an early night in preparation for lunch service, but the next day was harder than I could have imagined.

Moriyama-san had had plans that morning and rushed to the bistro just before noon. However, there was an influx of customers just before he arrived, and by that time I already had a full house on my hands.

Even though the couscous and the curry were the only things on the menu, for the first time since I'd started working at the bistro, I left our customers waiting for their food.

And if Murphy's Law suggested we'd be busier than usual on the day I happened to be holding the fort alone, there was no excuse for showing a group to a table that hadn't been fully cleaned and having to hurriedly wipe up with napkins, or rushing through plating up and serving dishes with sloppy presentation. I started to panic, and had to take deep breaths until I calmed down enough that my mind became quiet and clear, and I started to understand what I had to do, and in what order. That was when Moriyama-san arrived. I couldn't describe how relieved I was to see his round face and glasses come through the door. I could have hugged him.

I recounted my mistakes to him, feeling sorry for myself, and he consoled me, saying I'd done well for being all on my own.

For evening service, we wrote up the board outside to say we were running a limited menu, and with me and Moriyama-san working together, we just about managed to keep up. Even so, the plating and presentation fell short of our usual standards. By the time Shintani-kun came in just before closing, I had found my rhythm and acclimatized to the kitchen without

Michiyo-san in it. But that was too late—for many customers, that night would have been the only time they ate here.

I saw exactly how much I relied on Michiyo-san, day to day. How I'd thought I was standing on my own two feet, but actually might have only been slowing her down and getting in the way of her work.

Moriyama-san and I got through the next day's lunch service the same way.

When lunch was over, we got a phone call from Michiyo-san, who'd nearly lost her voice completely, saying she couldn't prep for dinner service, so we'd have to close. If we didn't open tomorrow, the day after that was our regular day off, so she'd get two more days of rest, which should be enough, she said.

I felt a little downcast, realizing I needed to be able to prep some simple stews at the very least if I wanted to keep the shop open in an emergency. I knew, of course, that I was nowhere near ready to take Michiyo-san's place, but I resolved to aim toward being able to keep the bistro going for a few days without her. I didn't intend to rush to learn many dishes, but to get a solid grasp on the basics so I could support her as best I could.

I'd moved so busily around the shop that by the time we closed, my legs felt like lumber, and I was unsteady on my feet.

Shintani-kun had waited for me, and we walked down the street in the dark looking for somewhere to have a drink. The cold air felt infinitely refreshing, and the stars glittered like pieces of ice. A strong wind was blowing, clearing the air, and every window into every building appeared sharp and close at hand.

"I thought I'd already been working as hard as I could, every day. But it turns out I'm still a child when it comes to what I can do. Plus I had more strength than I knew I had," I said. "I guess it's pretty childish in itself to not see yourself clearly until something like this happens."

"But no one could ever run a restaurant all alone. You'd have to be a child to think you could. And anyway, Yocchan, you're still in your twenties. It's too early to expect yourself to know how to keep cool and take care of everything," Shintani-kun said casually, yet sagely.

I had my arm hooked through his, and the woolen fabric of his expensive-looking duffel coat felt firm and dense and secure.

"I've got a long way to go," I said, but along with the sensation of my glowing cheeks cooling down, I was full of hope. I was aware that this was youth—the sheer joy of meeting new challenges and achieving things for the first time.

"Your nose is running," Shintani-kun said. He looked at me, then suddenly brought his gloved hand up and neatly wiped at my face.

"Stop it!" I said, and laughed, but Shintani-kun leaned straight in and kissed me hard. We were on Chazawa-Dori, which was nearly deserted at this hour of night, right outside the Showa Shinkin bank.

He held me tightly and pushed me against the closed shutters of the bank, and groped me all over.

"I'm not waiting any longer. Come stay tonight," Shintani-kun said.

"I'm exhausted, and I can't stay, but I can come back to yours if you like," I said.

"Let's go, then," he said, and hailed a taxi. *Why not?* I was thinking. I'd worked hard, and the bistro was going to be closed tomorrow.

In the taxi, I sat quietly. I wanted to think things through, but my attention kept flitting to things passing outside the window, and I didn't get very far. I wondered whether he'd mind that I knew nothing about his job or the sound system at his venue, and nor was I interested in learning. It was a strange thought, but I'd vaguely assumed he'd get married to someone he could run the business with. Or, if not, that he'd be against marriage because his parents were divorced.

Of course I'd gotten into the relationship knowing that we might split up, but I still felt sad about the possibility of it.

Just then, Shintani-kun said, artlessly, "I wish we could be there already," and I laughed out loud. I really loved discovering his sense of humor at moments like these, when it revealed itself in small and surprising ways.

Shintani-kun opened the front door to his dark apartment and turned on the light in the entry. I was taking off my coat and shoes in the now-familiar entry when he grabbed me and held me to him.

"Already?" I said.

"Already. Tea can wait," he said, "but I can't."

He probably couldn't, I thought, but I also thought he was used to not having to. He touched me, and it wasn't rough, or nervous—it felt very natural. We had sex for the first time on the sofa in his apartment, lit only by the light in the entry and the streetlights outside the window. Neither of us even took our clothes off.

Once you slept with someone, the distance between you suddenly grew a lot closer.

The milky late-night tea that Shintani-kun made us half an hour later, with clothes still mussed, tasted fantastic. He'd put loose Assam tea leaves into a pan of milk and simmered it, then added plenty of brown sugar. It was incredibly sweet and tasted of happiness. Then we laughed about how we'd originally planned to go for a drink, and got two cold beers out of his refrigerator and cracked them open.

The second time was much slower. We both undressed, and had sweet sex wrapped up in his woolen blanket. Shintani-kun's technique was eye-opening. I'd never experienced anything like it, and found myself almost looking forward to the next time.

Even so, somewhere inside, I knew we didn't have much of a future together.

I'd been vaguely aware of it before, but once we'd done it, there was nothing left between us. Nothing more for us to do—that was what it felt like. It was unbelievable, but it felt completely empty. I don't know whether Shintani-kun felt it too, or not. But I thought he did. Now that we had slept together, the spell had been broken.

"That was really lovely. See you soon," I said, wrapping up in my coat. Shintani-kun saw me to the road, still in his loungewear, and hailed me a taxi and waved until I couldn't see him anymore.

But I couldn't stop crying.

Why can't I love him? I wondered. *If only I could have done,* I thought. The taxi drove smoothly and silently toward Shimokitazawa through the dark streets. *Good-bye, my dead-end love. If we'd met at another time, I might have really fallen for you.*

The streets outside were swimming through my tears. I'd let it get this far because I'd been so scared to lose anything, because I wanted to keep things the same, I thought. I was lonely—I'd been lonely without him, that was why I'd been drawn to him. But I didn't love him. I could only ever come to like him a lot. I realized I'd known it all along, and had been trying to fool myself.

I SENT SHINTANI-KUN A message asking him to give me a little time, saying things had moved a little too quickly and I wasn't sure what I wanted. He wrote back, "Please feel free to get in touch anytime. I hope you will. I'll still go to the bistro—I can't picture life without it."

That was so typical of him; it made me laugh fondly.

I liked so many things about him, but I didn't think I'd ever be able to feel more than that. But I felt like I could keep that to myself a little longer, and still welcomed Shintani-kun coming by the bistro every two or three days. We kissed, or held hands, but nothing more. He was prepared to wait, and I was in no shape to make any definitive decisions. I was at my emotional limit finishing out my time at the restaurant. I was thankful that Shintani-kun understood and didn't press me to discuss anything deeper.

At the same time, though, a part of me knew this was because he'd done this all before. Not because he understood me, but because he knew from experience not to put pressure on a woman who was acting like I was.

It gave me a kind of shabby, inferior feeling—one that wasn't welcome in any way.

So that winter passed, and Les Liens's time in the Tsuyusaki Building came to an end. The date had been set for the demolition.

In those last days, our regulars all came through the door, one after the other, and every day was like a celebration.

On the very last night we held a small leaving party, and Shintani-kun and Mom came, and Michiyo-san and Moriyama-san both cried a little, and afterward we all cleared up for the final time, quietly. Our customers pitched in, too. We took a photograph of the view of Chazawa-Dori from the small window that had nurtured Mom's and my recovery in the early days, and carefully wiped down all the windowpanes. Then the building was locked up until the date when the movers were scheduled to come and take everything away.

"See you in France in February," Michiyo-san said as we parted outside the building, and disappeared into the darkness.

"The end of an era," Mom said, and the three of us—Mom, Shintani-kun, and me—went to Chizuru-san's bar to raise a toast to the bistro and my time there. I felt proud to have that celebrated by the two of them, plus Chizuru-san, who joined us for the toast.

Shintani-kun said he had to go, so Mom and I walked him to the station, and then strolled back through the shopping street.

The year was nearly over, and the streets were still busy even though it was late in the evening. I got the impression that people were rushing around wanting to draw some kind of line under the year, to mark the transition into the new one.

"You'll have some time on your hands from tomorrow; are you going to clean out the closet?" Mom said, smiling. "I'm kidding—you should take a break first."

"I will, thanks. Hey, Mom?" I said, and then realized I didn't know what I wanted to talk about. I eventually settled on, "What do you think of me and Shintani-kun?"

Mom looked at me for a second, and we walked on in silence for a little while. Her pointy boots clicked distinctly on the ground. When we got around halfway down the street, outside Sunkus, she finally said, "You seem like . . . friends who've slept together. No offense, but it doesn't feel like you'll get married, or anything major like that. Even though he's great."

"Right," I said. It was the answer I'd been expecting.

I could tell Mom had answered carefully, knowing her opinion would carry a lot of weight with me, and I loved her for that.

"I'm sorry. To be pessimistic when you're in the middle of your love affair," she said sincerely, as though she was talking to a good friend.

"No, I was kind of thinking along the same lines," I said. "Do you think I should come clean with him?"

"I don't think you need to feel like you should do anything," said Mom. "Like the old saying goes—*kenka ryoseibai*. Fight and you both lose."

"I'm pretty sure that's not what it means," I said, laughing, "but I know exactly what you're saying."

Over the past few weeks, I'd been wrapped up in the things I needed to do to get through each day at the bistro, and put off dealing with the idea of it closing until it actually happened so that the end had come almost as a surprise. Toward the end, we were so busy that Moriyama-san had come in most days, which actually made the rush feel almost enjoyable.

Now that it was really over, I felt a little let down. Then, out of nowhere, I thought—*If Dad hadn't died, that woman would have found someone else to kill. Which means Dad saved someone from being her next victim. How hard might things have been if Dad had survived and the next person had died in his place?*

For the first time, I truly understood what it meant for the customer from Ibaraki to have come to see me.

"Mom, there's something I want to tell you," I said. "Can we head to that fancy bar for another drink? My treat."

"Sure. Is it about your love life?" Mom said.

"No, it's about a lady who came by the shop a while ago," I said.

"Okay," Mom said. She probably knew from my expression what it was about.

WE SAT AT THE bar and ordered our usual cocktails garnished with seasonal fresh fruit, and I told Mom the whole story— how I'd met with Yamazaki-san, and been given the bag of salt by the customer who'd come to Les Liens and the talismans by Shintani-kun, and the things I'd discovered about that woman.

Once I'd unburdened myself, I realized my secret had been pretty trivial, and I'd been building it up into more of a problem than it was. Mom didn't seem that upset either, only frowning occasionally.

Mom looked really beguiling when she furrowed her brow, and I thought that must have been how she'd looked when she was young.

"So, what do you want to do about it?" Mom said. "Go to that forest and make offerings, or give prayers, or something? Like in that book *The Mourner*?"

"I didn't know you kept up with the latest best sellers," I said.

"I have plenty of time on my hands," she said, "even working part-time."

"Anyway, I'm not exactly sure. But I'm wondering if we should," I said.

"Sorry, but I'm not interested," Mom said. "Because we'd be praying for that woman's soul, too. Anyway, I haven't accepted it all enough yet, so it would be a lie."

"I thought you'd say that. So I just wanted to mention it," I said, but my eyes started to tear up. It was strange, like being a child again. That I'd cry just because Mom had rejected me.

"I'm sorry, Yocchan. But I think we should agree to be separate on this," she said. "I don't actually hate her anymore. I feel like she won, but it was careless of me to let her steal him. And more careless of Dad to let her take his life. Still, that doesn't mean I'm happy to put my hands together and hope she makes it to the afterlife."

"Of course, that's fair enough," I said, wiping away the tears spilling out of my eyes.

"I need to stand my ground and do what's right for me," Mom said. "You're the only one in the world I share this with. So if you say you want to go back to the forest, I won't stop you. But I don't want to, and I need to honor my feeling about that. I don't think I'll ever go. I'm happy with where I'm at now, thinking back on the nice memories or things I loved about him from time to time."

"Yeah, I know. It's not like I'm still a child and want you to come with me, or need you to kneel next to me so we can pray together. I'm prepared to keep on feeling conflicted about things. It's just that Dad keeps calling me on the phone in my dreams, so I feel like I need to do something about it," I said.

"Yeah, you should do what you think best," Mom said. "I don't mind, and I'm not against it. I just have no desire to go with you. I don't want to do anything so clean, so neat. It's healthier for me to keep hold of this quivering resentment.

"But don't think I'm ungrateful. I don't remember a lot about the early days, even though I tried to pull myself together. I felt like my mind had gone dark, and the days just passed me by. I know I leaned on you a lot, with moving in and everything. I can't express how much of a support you were to me, Yocchan.

"Can you understand what it's like to be abandoned like this? It's pretty pathetic even as appearances go, but I'm not talking about that. People were kind enough to say Dad couldn't have been serious about her, that he must have been manipulated into it. But that's not the point. You despise yourself. You feel disgusting and unwanted, and want to disappear. Every time anything even slightly good starts to happen, you instantly see their bodies lying there dead, together. And then your mind starts conjuring up images of them getting into bed together, or drinking together, and you start to feel completely worthless, totally meaningless.

"When I was with you, Yocchan, that was the only time I could feel like I had any value in the world. I'm so glad we decided to have you. We'd kind of reached a dead end, Dad and I, and we talked about either calling it quits or starting over and having a baby, and we decided to try. I know it was absolutely the right decision. I can't imagine life without you, you're the most important thing in my life—that you're safe, and you can live your life. It's far more important to me than mine.

"But even after all that, I can't go back there to the forest, with you and your pure feelings. I live with too much murkiness inside me to do that. I catch myself wishing he'd die, all the time. But he'll never be deader than he already is," she said.

I nodded and sipped my cocktail. The taste of fresh fruit spread over my tongue. This was all that being alive meant, really.

It wasn't that I'd been a good daughter. There were many times I'd resented Mom, if only mildly, for having tumbled into my apartment and my life. I also resented Shintani-kun for wanting me all the time, and how I could work as hard as I liked at the bistro but it was never going to be mine, I could serve customers with all my heart but it wasn't as though they were going to do anything for me, and nor would Michiyo-san marry me and secure my future career. I could easily have found reasons to believe that everything was futile, that I was being taken advantage of, losing out, sacrificing myself for people around me.

But something that Mom and Dad had given me had stopped me from doing that.

I felt that they'd somehow taught me, through their actions, to be proud of being loved.

They'd lived their own lives, true to themselves, even if that meant meeting a foolish end, or running away from home and moving in with their daughter. That kept me true.

Just then, gaze distant, glass in hand, Mom said something that made my hair stand on end.

"About those dreams? I have them, too. I know he wanted to call. It was the only thing on his mind when he died. I know it's true, like I was holding it in my hand. And it wasn't that woman he wanted to talk to, even though she was right there—it was us. So that's enough, actually. It's fine. It's enough for me."

THAT NIGHT, SUDDENLY RELIEVED of both the burden of keeping secrets from Mom and the pressure of not getting sick during the restaurant's last days, I came down with a fever. It was a textbook case of so-called thinking fever—my temperature shot up, only to subside about three hours later.

I lay under the covers, sipping on water. Mom made me a hot drink with honey and lemon, and I drank it down, shivering. As the sourness made its way into my cells, I found myself strangely disturbed by the dirt on the old tatami mats. Things like that were more visible when you were feverish. Even so, I still didn't want to go back to the spotless rooms of the condo. That had been our family's home. That time was over.

"So I'm still in a Yusaku Matsuda phase. I'll keep the volume down," Mom said, and started watching *A Homansu* on the TV.

The young Satomi Tezuka looked like an angel to my fevered eyes.

The light from the TV dappling the dark room made me think of family vacations of old. I felt as though I was back in a room in a traditional inn, already asleep, while Mom and Dad watched TV lounging on the mat floor.

When I thought of that I started crying ordinary tears, probably for the first time since it had all happened. It wasn't

weeping, or wailing, or cursing, or suffering, or hate, or regret.
They were tears that marveled that I wasn't a child any longer,
and lamented the time that had passed since I had been. They
flowed and flowed on and on, endlessly.

Mom and I had got so used to each other crying wordlessly
in that little apartment that she noticed me crying, and didn't
say a word. Neither cold nor hot, she was simply there in the
same space, feeling for me.

When I realized that, I knew that I was happy.

It was a different happiness from the frivolous happiness
of eating grilled meat with a newish boyfriend. I felt myself
being accepted and forgiven and redeemed on a far more fundamental level.

I woke up, looked at my clock, and thought, *I'm late!* until
I thought about it and remembered that the bistro no longer
existed. I couldn't believe I had nothing else to do until after
New Year. It was as though my body still hadn't caught up
with the facts and wanted to go to work. Like I'd left a part of
me somewhere.

Mom had gone out already, and I found some rice porridge
in a pan on the stove. I wondered whether she'd made porridge
because I'd been sick and crying last night.

The winter sky was clear and blue, and the wind was whistling though the air. The tatami mats shone in the white sunlight
as though it had bleached them.

Savoring the sweet taste of the rice porridge, I looked down
through the window at the now-darkened bistro, and felt conflicted. It wasn't just closed—it was never going to come alive

with customers again. In a few days' time, contractors would come in to remove the equipment from the kitchen. Everything that could still be used was temporarily going to Michiyo-san's parents' house. Michiyo-san was heading off to France mid-January, and I was joining her in February. We'd made a date to meet up in Paris and start our journey off in an oyster bar. I had a few things to take care of until then—renewing my passport, getting my suitcases from the house in Meguro—but right now, I wasn't thinking about any of it yet.

The sky was high, and I felt as though I might be able to float away into it like a kite.

I suddenly thought about going to Ibaraki. I'd take the salt, and the talismans, and make it there while it was still light. I felt like it might be possible on a day like today, when the sky was clear, and I felt empty.

I gathered what I needed, and texted Mom: *Fever's down. Heading to Ibaraki to give prayers for Dad. Planning to be back late tonight.* Then I left the apartment.

I got to Tokyo Station and bought a ticket for the bus, and some rice balls and tea from the food court. I had fifteen minutes before the bus departed, so I sat on a bench and watched the concourse and the buses leaving for various destinations, and the quiet, meek passengers as they got on board, and suddenly felt so lonely I could hardly stand it. I didn't know why, but I started crying, and I felt like I couldn't breathe, and I didn't know what to do. *No,* I thought, *I've got to pull myself together so I can get on the bus,* but the more I thought, the more I felt the loneliness suffocating me. A strange sensation was coming over me, like I'd lost everything.

I'll call Mom, after all, I thought, and got out my cell phone. I had a missed call. I thought it might have been Shintani-kun, but when I checked, it was Yamazaki-san. I called him back almost reflexively.

"*Moshi moshi*," Yamazaki-san answered. Even in my panic, his voice seemed to calm me.

"I apologize for missing your call," I said, politely, even though my voice was nasal from crying, and I was still swallowing sobs.

"I was wondering about the Ibaraki business. Since it was sunny today, I thought it might be a nice day for it. Oh, I'm not suggesting we go today, or anything, it just gave me the idea," Yamazaki-san said, breezily.

"Let's go today," I said, crying. "I'm actually at Tokyo Station right now, and I'm about to get the bus to Suigo Itako. But I'm sad and I can't stop crying, and I want to take someone with me."

"Wait, you're there now? And, crying?" Yamazaki-san said. "What about your mother?"

"She turned me down," I said. "I couldn't talk her around. She said no."

I felt even lonelier, and the tears welled up, and I wept down the phone at Yamazaki-san. He didn't say anything for a good few minutes while I just cried. Then, he said, "That's fine, let's go. I'm free today, and it sounds like fun. You're about to get on the bus? I'll drive, and catch you up."

I was in awe. I said meekly, "Yes, I'll wait. If we could keep in touch between Suigo Itako and Kashima, I think we should be able to find each other." I had nothing more to lose.

"I think you'll get there ahead of me," he said.

"In that case, I'll go to Sante and have a soak in the hot spring," I said.

"Fine, I'll look it up and follow the sat-nav. I'll call you when I get there," he said.

I was so impressed by his decisiveness that I felt a surge of admiration which felt very close to attraction. My heart, which had felt totally lost only a few minutes ago, felt warm, and I boarded the bus feeling hopeful.

I realized then that I'd desperately wanted Mom to come with me.

I'd assumed that once I'd passed the age of twenty, I'd gained the power to do everything alone. But I'd been wrong about that, and this just brought it home to me, again, that I still had a long way to go. The sense of failure, however, was a strangely comfortable one—the feeling of looking up and starting over again after pride and defensiveness had slipped away, and left me soft and crumpled on the ground.

The bus set off and joined the highway. I dozed off, and before long, we had reached the bus station at Suigo Itako. The last time I'd been here, I hadn't taken in any of my surroundings, and remembered it as a desolate place, like a windswept field. But now I could. I saw the dry wind crossing the sky, far and high in the distance. I saw wide expanses of grass, with the occasional patch that shone gold. The view looked altogether different when I looked at it with a calm eye.

From there, I took a taxi to the spa where I'd arranged to meet Yamazaki-san.

The spa complex was just off the main road and faced out toward the ocean. Like a tourist, I put my luggage into a locker, and scrubbed myself among the local old ladies in the women's bath, and then soaked in the spacious open-air hot spring to my heart's content, watching the vast blue sky and the wild sea that lay distantly beyond the trees. It had been a while since I'd last seen anything this big and spacious, and I felt my heart open in response. I was glad I'd come.

I finally admitted to myself that this whole time, I'd been in a phase where I was more in love with Yamazaki-san than I was with Shintani-kun. The realization felt good. I was glad to know I was never going to like Shintani-kun enough to want to marry him. The way he hadn't been able to wait that night was the best thing about him, and I was in no position to appreciate it.

If only he could have waited a little longer, I thought, things might have turned out differently. With all his experience with women, I simply hadn't been able to trust him when it counted. I felt that if I let my body go ahead and get closer to him, my heart would get left further and further behind.

Trust Mom to understand, I thought. Why had she been watching *Detective Story*, anyway? The movie, to boot, rather than the TV series. The answer had been there all along.

I got out of the hot spring after an hour or so, and found a text on my cell phone, saying: *I've arrived, but can't reach you, so I'm heading to the bath. Let's meet in the main hall.*

I went to the main hall and lounged on the tatami mats, and was dozing off when Yamazaki-san came in fresh from the hot spring, as though we were family members who'd come here together.

"Hi, Yocchan," he said.

From where I was lying, I looked up at Yamazaki-san's big, round eyes, and found a safe place for me inside them. A strange calm took over me. In his eyes I saw a space I could enter easily into, which went beyond logic or reason. I hadn't been wrong—it had nothing to do with how many times we'd met, what had happened, or what he'd done for me. I was attracted to this man, I thought. Even if he had a beautiful wife, and would never find out I had feelings for him.

I got up. "I'm sorry I wasn't answering my phone," I said. "And I'm sorry for asking you to come all the way out here."

"I'd kill for a post-bath beer, but I'm driving," Yamazaki-san smiled. "Don't worry about it. I was at a loose end today, and I agreed to come because I wanted to."

How old was he? I wondered, and worked out that he must be around forty-five. He was younger than Dad, but had seemed older, since he was so placid. Close up, his skin was youthful, and I blithely wondered whether his clothes didn't also add to the impression.

"You know, I saw how the wind was today, and the sky, and it made me think I should go and visit Imo's grave today, so I gave you a call. I didn't plan on coming all the way out here, but I'm not complaining. On a day as full of light as today, the chances of reaching the afterlife must be pretty good, wouldn't you say?" Yamazaki-san said.

I watched his quintessentially middle-aged profile as he spoke, and felt more safe and more comfortable than ever. That was what had happened to me, too, I thought. The sky today had made me think the same.

"Yes, I wanted to get it over with," I said. I decided to stop acting helpless, or like I needed him. I decided to meet him as an equal. "Like I couldn't move forward unless I did. I had the talismans and the salt in my bag, just getting heavier and heavier. But when Mom said no, I felt much more alone than I'd expected. So I was glad you could come. To tell the truth, I was terrified of going back there. Thank you for coming with me," I said.

"I feel like you've grown up a lot, Yocchan, in a really short time," Yamazaki-san said.

"No, some things that happened made me realize that I'd been acting like a child," I said.

THE PLACE WHERE DAD and that woman had committed suicide was near a small crop of houses in a forest, a long way from the main road.

It was at the end of a little-used gravel road, which started in an area of abandoned-looking houses—with wooden decks which were rotting and falling down, or broken windows—and cottages with surfboards leaning on them outside that looked like they were only used in summer. The road was overgrown with dense branches stretching out from the forest on either side, limiting visibility.

Dad (and that woman) had been found by a woman who lived locally. She and her husband, who was a picture-book author, had moved to the area and were some of the few people who lived there year-round. She'd noticed that the car had been parked at the end of a dead-end road for a long time, and had checked on it when she walked her dog.

This woman seemed very kind, and had genuinely taken pity on Mom and me when we'd arrived on the scene, and given us hot cups of tea. Later, we sent her a box of sweets by way of thanks, and she replied with a truly kind letter. Her husband had also included a wonderful drawing.

Remembering that couple, I reflected that even that devastating day had contained a ray of light. We were in Yamazaki-san's beat-up Mini Cooper, driving deeper into the forest with the wind whistling through the trees. The car was bumpy to ride in at the best of times, and going up and down the hills on the unsurfaced road, it felt like being on a roller coaster.

The two of us gradually fell silent.

I was giving Yamazaki-san directions to the spot, but I started to feel short of breath, and dizzy. I asked myself if I was really going back there.

Of course, Dad's car wasn't there any longer—I wouldn't be met with that terrible sight again. Now there was only an empty, dead-end lane covered in fallen leaves.

What a hateful place, I thought. Dad had died there, had reached the end his life, and not willingly. All his music, and his work, and his time with us—everything had been sucked into that desolate black hole of a place and disappeared.

"This is it," I said.

Yamazaki-san stopped the car. We got out, and I said, "If I left the talismans here, the local residents probably wouldn't be that thrilled, don't you think?"

"I'm sure it would be alright. Couldn't you bury them in the ground, even?" Yamazaki-san said.

"Yes, I think I'll bury them over here out of the way," I said.

Yamazaki-san got a spade out of the back of the car. It was definitely a spade, and not a trowel.

"What did you use that for, and when?" I asked.

"A long time ago. I think it was when my wife planted some bulbs in her folks' garden," Yamazaki-san said, laughing.

"And how is she?" I said.

"We got divorced. Two years ago. She left," Yamazaki-san said. "Oh, it wasn't because I wasn't faithful, or anything. There was a bit of that, but she was just a very unhappy person. And we wanted kids but couldn't conceive. She found herself a young boyfriend, divorced me, married him, and has a late-in-life baby now."

To be completely honest, when he said that, I did feel a small spark of hope. But I assumed, knowing him, that he was with someone else by now.

"I see," I said. "I'm sure it can't have been easy, with someone that beautiful. But I'm sorry to hear it. You were a lovely couple—I thought so, and Mom did, too."

"So Imo's gone, and I'm divorced, and a lot of things have changed in the last couple of years. I'm almost surprised I'm still here, carrying on," Yamazaki-san said.

"I feel like I've lost everything, too, even though I've still got Mom," I said.

"That's because you think about everything in words," Yamazaki-san said. "You can go around and around the same questions all you like, and never find an answer. Yocchan, I know that's how you cope, how you get through time, so I've never thought it was immature, or unhelpful. But there's another way of doing it: to sit with an empty space, and just look at it, without thinking anything, just enduring. Some people can do that. I think your mom is one of those."

He was right, so I stayed quiet.

"When you see your mom like that, you must get worried, and feel like you need to think about things for her. I can understand that. But you can't think for someone, no matter how close you are. Even though I think that's one of the great things about you, and I like it very much. You always try so hard, thinking and working and taking care of people all the time, being so brave it makes me feel like I might cry," he said.

"I know, if I could have used all the time and energy I spent just thinking to generate electricity or something, I'm sure that would have been a lot more useful," I said. "But it really was the only thing I could have done about this. I don't think I've ever thought about anything so much."

"No, I think you've always thought a lot for other people, ever since you were young. Both Imo and your mom were more the type to try things first, and think later. It was always you thinking about the two of them. But they never really paid any attention, did they? I used to see it and think how tough it was to be an only child. You were always worrying about them, saying things like, 'Dad, Mom, won't you have a fever tomorrow if you do that? If you eat so much, won't it give you a stomachache later?'" Yamazaki-san said. "It might be time to start putting yourself first."

"Thank you, Yamazaki-san," I said, sincerely thankful to have been seen, and for what he'd said.

Then we started digging. I felt slightly guilty for burying the talismans since they'd been consecrated, but thought maybe the offense was minimal compared to what Dad and the woman had done. But then it dawned on me that the gods probably didn't feel that inconvenienced by anything we humans could do, even far more major things—even suicide or murder. When I thought of it that way, I felt a little better.

I placed the talismans Shintani-kun had given me into the ground, thanking him silently as I did.

Then I took out the other thing I'd brought with me: Dad's cell phone—the phone that had appeared so many times in my dreams.

After Dad had left his phone at home that morning, it had stayed there at the condo, charging, even after he was dead, until the police had come and taken it away saying they'd give it a once-over. There were lots of texts and calls from that woman, of course, as well as the innocent, everyday texts from Mom and me. We were tormented for a long time by the thought that if only Dad hadn't left his phone behind that day, if he'd gotten in touch at some point, we might have noticed that something was going on, and might have been able to stop him. The night the police returned the phone, wrapped in a plastic bag, Mom threw it against the floor of the entry in the condo and stomped all over it in fury. Then she threw herself down on the floor and wept loudly. I saw that and started crying, too, set off by her tears. Mom cried and yelled about how she didn't want to see what was on the phone, and that she was angry the police had seen into our life.

So that cracked and broken phone was completely destroyed, about as dead as Dad, but when I'd picked it up from the floor of the entry, I hadn't quite felt able to get rid of it, and had kept it around.

I buried the phone with the talismans. I felt a little guilty to Dad that I was burying his phone, but I wanted to, because it would always make me sad. I had enough things that reminded me of him, I didn't need to keep one that hurt so much.

I also hoped that once it was buried, Dad might stop looking for it in my dreams.

Sweetly, gently, I said in my heart: *Dad, your phone's spirit is on its way over to you, so you can call us all you want now.* Then I moved the fallen leaves back over the spot.

"Is that Imo's phone? I recognize it. How'd it get so broken? It must have been really violent," Yamazaki-san said. Then he laughed, and said, "Why are you covering it up with leaves again like that? It's not a booby trap, you know."

The way he said it was so funny that somehow, it made me laugh, too. The sound of our laughter traveled lightly on the wind and floated out through the trees.

Then I opened the pouch of salt, and gave some to Yamazaki-san, too, and we scattered it around as though we were doing a purification.

Then we put our hands together and prayed.

Dad, we've got your photograph safe in Shimokitazawa. You can leave this world behind now. Mom might still be a little angry, but I'm pretty sure she doesn't really blame anyone anymore.

And . . . strange, beautiful, unhappy woman, who—I don't know if it's because my aunt, who's pretty good-looking, was a bit of a wild thing in her youth? Not that it really matters—circumstances have conspired to connect us so deeply: I don't know a lot about you, nor do I want to, but I'm praying for you, too. If you get born again, don't kill yourself, or anyone else. I can kind of sympathize with not wanting to die alone, but you've given us a lot to deal with. You certainly changed my life.

"That's better," Yamazaki-san said, and I quickly opened my eyes.

I realized he was only speaking for himself, how he felt better, and I was glad for that.

Just like it was the right thing for Mom not to come, it wouldn't have been right for me to be praying while someone was there just waiting around for me to finish, either.

I got up, thinking I'd probably never come here again, even if I might visit his grave at some point. I bowed my toward the lights in the distance, which belonged to the home of the picture book author and his wife.

May you live long and well, and be happy. Thank you for all you've done for us.

"I feel a little better, too. When I thought about this place, I kept seeing Dad's car parked here, and the police cars, and it made me feel so dark and scared. I think it'll be easier for me now that I have the memory of today on top of that," I said. I'd felt calm, but there were tears rolling down my face.

Just a few moments earlier, as I'd been on the verge of leaving this place behind forever, I'd suddenly remembered how warm that tea the picture book artist's wife had made for us that day had been. She'd smiled, and handed it to us cheerfully, while her husband had quietly looked on from behind her. His eyes had a depth that came of having seen many things, and spoke of the years that they had traveled together as husband and wife. They must have been shocked and repulsed, too, but they met us solidly, and cared for us without giving even a hint of it. Mom and I had drunk the tea down, momentarily forgetting everything else. The tea had tasted unforgettable. It had tasted of kindness—an unconditional human kindness that didn't demand anything in return, and which I'd desperately wanted to cling to.

"In that case I'm glad," Yamazaki-san said. He looked at his watch. "It's already four. We didn't make it to the aquarium. But I guess the hot spring made up for it."

"No, let's still go," I said. My heart was hammering. I felt myself blush. "First thing tomorrow morning."

"Yocchan, what are you saying?" Yamazaki-san said. "Imo would kill me."

"He can't, because he's already dead," I said.

"He'll come back and possess me, and then kill me," Yamazaki-san said, and smiled. I saw his neat teeth and thought, *He has the best smile.* It made the bleak winter forest surrounding us sparkle.

"I don't mind if nothing happens," I said. "I just want to let myself go and have some fun. It's all I can do right now."

Yamazaki-san didn't say anything. I stuck my hands in my pockets and looked up into the sky in the distance. "I don't mind if something does happen, either," I said. "I'm not anyone's. Plus, I want to experience the thing that killed Dad for myself—the forces that take hold between a man and a woman."

Yamazaki-san looked at me gravely. After a while, he said, "Yocchan, any middle-aged man who didn't like you, who didn't care for you, would want to have you in bed. That's how men work. But if I were to do anything to you, I'd hate myself tomorrow. I couldn't live with that. So please don't say that kind of thing."

I nodded. I couldn't stop crying, and I liked Yamazaki-san even more than I had done before, and I felt cheated.

"Am I allowed to like you?" I said.

"You're in no shape to get to liking anyone properly," he said. "And any man who doesn't understand that, or will take advantage of it, is a fool."

I nearly said, *Apparently a man can understand it but still not be able to help himself,* but I didn't.

"I think you're right. I might just be looking for someone to lean on," I said. "Maybe that's just what happens when there's no longer a man in the house."

Yamazaki-san laughed. "I shouldn't laugh, but you're funny, Yocchan," he said.

"Then let's go to Oarai aquarium, some other time. Will you take me there? Mom can come if she wants, and we'll make it a day trip. I just didn't want this to be my only memory of today," I said. "And Dad loved aquariums, so I wanted to go for him."

"Sure, we can do that once it gets a little warmer, and ask your mom, too. But let's head back for now. We've got to have a celebration to send him off. We'll go back to Tokyo, and I'll drop the car. We'll have some sake, and something to eat. Let's push the boat out and treat ourselves," he said.

"If we can split the bill," I said.

"Imo would beat me up for that, too," he said, and smiled.

"If you're going to get beaten up just by seeing me, what does it matter?" I said, and laughed, and forgave myself for asking too much, and felt satisfied.

Of course, I was still forlorn.

The spot where Dad had died was still a desolate, isolated, lonely, and hopeless kind of place, and we still didn't know anything about that woman who'd died with him, or even how he'd felt about things. But that was probably just how things went. The sky was still clear, and the air was fresh, and my days went on, and Mom was alive. No one's true feelings could ever be known, or pinned down. There was no need for answers. Nothing was the same now as it had been that terrible day.

If I went somewhere upsetting, I'd grieve, and if I went to eat good food with someone I liked who was still alive, I'd have fun—that was all. I didn't need to know how Dad had felt. There was a lot I'd loved about him, and that was all I could ever be certain of.

Sure it was ambiguous, and annoying, and frustrating, and murky, and worrisome, and none of us was doing everything right, but maybe that was all okay.

It was fine, I thought. It didn't really matter, it was all fine.

Because I was alive, and I was with someone I probably really loved.

When I truly grasped that idea, in that forest as dark fell around us, I finally understood how Mom had felt when she'd tumbled into my apartment all those months ago. I was able to make sense of her actions not as those of a parent, but as a fellow human being.

Peace and acceptance suddenly fell into my hands. Like a patch of rich soil that had soaked up plenty of sun mounding gently up into an empty space, I felt something akin to an answer settle in me.

HAVING PAID OUR RESPECTS, Yamazaki-san and I both suddenly felt very hungry, and we got in his car, chatting like old friends about how sake seemed most appropriate after any kind of memorial, and what we should eat to go with it. We joined the highway feeling calm and at peace.

I could tell that my confession had untangled another thing that had been between us, and that both of us were now feeling more at ease, and more happy. As we talked and he drove, I felt he was truly accepting me for who I was.

It might just have been Yamazaki-san's kindness and experience letting me feel that way, but I felt like we might genuinely be extremely compatible, given how much we were enjoying ourselves just through spending time together.

I found out that thanks to the influence of his ex-wife, Yamazaki-san was uncompromising when it came to food. After a lot of impassioned discussion, he mentioned an incredibly good soba-noodle restaurant near his house and we decided to go there. We were genuinely excited, almost like we'd forgotten that we'd just been to visit the scene where someone had died, or as though we'd discussed it beforehand and agreed this would be the best way to put it behind us.

We talked about memories of Dad, and Mom's quirks, and Yamazaki-san's divorce, and though we were making an effort to keep the conversation light and casual, the calm and hopeful atmosphere remained steady around us.

The only time I felt like crying was when the radio station we were tuned to started playing a song that Shintani-kun had put on his stereo for me the first time I'd gone to his apartment.

Being with Shintani-kun had been a lot of fun, and part of me wished I could have stayed in that illusion forever.

But I knew now that I shouldn't see him again. Now that I knew who I was happiest with—even if it was only in a limited way based on things that had happened in the past, or maybe just a temporary, one-sided crush on my part—I couldn't see him anymore.

We might be able to be friends one day, I thought. If he wanted to. But that would be a long time in the future. We wouldn't be going drinking together after work again—when I thought of that, I felt genuine sadness. Things that didn't work out had their own abortive, fleeting charm.

The song on the radio affected me differently than when I'd heard it the first time. In a weak, transparent voice, the singer crooned: *Just one more time.*

I'd spent my days with no regrets. I wasn't sorry I'd slept with Shintani-kun, either. But I had no choice but to move forward into my new life. *Good-bye, my Les Liens/Shintani-kun period! You were gone before I knew it, like sand falling through my fingers.*

The verdant views to either side of the highway slipped away behind us about just as quickly as my feelings did.

THE SOBA PLACE THAT Yamazaki-san liked was closer to a traditional *kappo* restaurant than a simple noodle bar. It was the kind of place where a procession of numerous small dishes of sophisticated cooking was rounded off by a final plate of splendid handmade buckwheat noodles. I recalled Michiyo-san telling me that there were so many of this type of restaurant cropping up recently, she couldn't keep up trying to visit them all. Traditional buckwheat noodles might seem unlikely to feature at a French-inspired bistro, but Michiyo-san was always on the lookout for good food, and ate at all kinds of places for research. *I'll have to tell her about this place,* I thought, and then felt dumbfounded that Les Liens would still be gone tomorrow.

At times like this I realized just how much I had come to rely on having the bistro as a cornerstone of my life, and how much it had meant for me to have found a place for myself there.

While Yamazaki-san went to drop his car back at home, I killed some time in a bookstore opposite the station. I was waiting for him near the new releases when he arrived smiling, having changed his outfit just slightly. Spending the day with him like this, I felt as though he was someone I'd been seeing for a long time—even though I knew that this was only an illusion, and that I'd go back to not seeing him for weeks or months at a time come tomorrow.

In the soba restaurant, we were shown to a low table in a private tatami-matted room. We drank a little sake, and ate some good food.

"This really ought to be my treat," I said, frankly, "since you so kindly agreed to accompany me today. But this restaurant is very expensive, and the best I can do is to split the check."

"I'm the one who suggested this place," Yamazaki-san said. "I was trying to impress you, so let me get it. I thought we should go for something fancier than ramen or *yakiniku,* since you're a professional, after all. And having gone all that way earlier to an area famed for seafood and then having turned back without tasting any, I got it into my head that we should come here to make up for it. Take me out next time we go somewhere—maybe the aquarium. I wish we could have gone today. I do enjoy a good aquarium.

"My favorite part of the one at Oarai is the big shark tank. Oh, and the strange jungle gym near the end, it's quite a brilliant design. When I see the kids playing on it I get so emotional, I feel like I might cry," he said.

"Let's make it happen, before summer comes. I wanted to see it, too. Aquariums are only open during the day, right? We can set off early next time. Thank you for the fantastic meal. It'll be my treat when we go to the aquarium. Maybe a monkfish hotpot," I said.

At times like these, I felt grateful that the last conversation I'd had with Dad had been a happy one. Making plans to eat good food together was always a happy thing.

The soba noodles arrived to round off the meal, and we both became too busy tucking in to say anything more. I found it charming how Yamazaki-san slurped his noodles almost silently. We talked a little about how he used to feel really self-conscious about his noodle-slurping prowess. Then he said, "Does your mom know you've been talking to me about your dad?"

"She does. Which means that us going to the aquarium together isn't suspicious at all," I said.

"You're two steps ahead of me," Yamazaki-san said, and laughed.

"That doesn't mean I'm grown up," I said. "I still want to throw a tantrum and say, *I don't want today to end. I don't want to go home.*"

"That again," Yamazaki-san said.

"I'm sorry, I know," I said. "You knew me as a child. Of course you can't, I understand that. I'm just pushing my luck, in a childish way. I'll go back to my immature world. But let's meet again."

I felt very at peace. I had the satisfied feeling of knowing I'd done all I could. I felt like I had nothing more to be scared of, and nothing more to lose.

"Earlier," Yamazaki-san said. He'd pulled his legs out from under the table, and sat leaning forward with his legs crossed. We were still drinking sake, and he had a circle of red on his cheek, like a spot of rouge—not because he was embarrassed by the topic, but from the drink. I found this endearing, too. I saw again that he was a younger man than Dad, and not yet spent. The skin was different, the lines on his hands were different. Dad had been a lot more tired of life.

"Yes," I said.

"You mentioned something about wanting to understand the power that took your dad away. What did you mean by that? Something like the inescapable bonds that tie a couple to each other?" he said.

"Yes. I guess I feel like I might be able to forgive him if it was something so strong it made you feel that everything else was unimportant. But I've never experienced it," I said.

"Imo was timid . . . and a dreamer, I mean useless at practical things," said Yamazaki-san. "He went to a doctor complaining about stomach pain, and they found a small tumor. It was cancer. He came to me about it.

"They said he could live for years if they operated. It wasn't an aggressive form. If they'd operated promptly, they might have got rid of it altogether. I even found him a good specialist. But he never told his family, right? He was such a child when it came to things like that. He probably felt that that telling you would make it all real," he said.

"Wow . . . I had no idea," I said. "What a shock. I wonder if Mom knew. I should tell her."

"Yes, I suppose it might be all right to tell her, now. Or perhaps she already knows," Yamazaki-san said. "I think he stopped caring about a lot of things, because of that, and he ran away. He didn't want to have anything to do with hospitals, or tests, or anything, just like a child. What an idiot. Really."

"I wonder if he got sick because of that woman," I said.

"Oh, did you think so, too? That was the first thing that came to my mind. It goes to show—I'm not sure how to say this, but we don't really know anything about her, do we? We never met her, or talked to her. That's probably why we think these things—us, and the lady who brought you the salt, as well, I think we've all projected some kind of big, dark, and menacing image onto that woman.

"Some kind of vast darkness, something like a myth. Certainly, there was something about her that evoked that. But I think as a person, she was just an unfortunate woman, only a fraction of the idea we have in our minds.

"We've all been forced to confront something big and dark and mysterious through the lens of Imo's incomprehensible death. But isn't that what most of life is like? And that's so frightening that we all cast around for things that are simple, things we can easily understand.

"So I think maybe the reason we feel like they must have been having uninhibited, mind-blowing, better-than-life sex is because we want an explanation, we want to make things make sense. I'm middle-aged now, so I know a little more about it than you do, but I'm pretty sure it wasn't just that Imo fell for some woman and drowned," he said.

I fell silent.

I thought again about Dad—the proud, insecure mama's boy with a shadow side who'd hidden his weaknesses from Mom, and had tried to always appear the good father to me.

"What a stupid thing to do," I said.

"I agree," Yamazaki-san said.

"That revelation has chased away my sexy thoughts completely," I said. "And I've lost my appetite, too. I'm glad I already ate that delicious soba." Something deep inside my chest felt like it was being squeezed tightly.

"Not for me," said Yamazaki-san. "I'm starting to feel I've had enough of being the kindly older man. Like I might be interested in being the rogue.

"I'm feeling drawn to you, Yocchan. That's about what men are like, I think. There's no glory in pretending otherwise, trying to look good, and getting drunk on my own self-restraint. Plus, your head—it might just be youth, I don't know—it's far too full of words. I know there's nothing I can really do about that, but I can't help but want to empty it out for you. To tell the truth, I've been wavering since a little while ago," he said.

"Are men really *that* different from women?!" I asked, astonished by this sudden development.

"I think they are," Yamazaki-san said. His calm voice made a strong impression on me. The more I listened to him, the more grounded I felt, and the more sharply my feelings came into focus. *What was happening?* I wondered.

The total bill for the small dishes and the soba, when I overheard it, was tremendously expensive. I realized just how much Yamazaki-san had splurged on treating me, but if I insisted on paying half, I wouldn't have enough money to make it home. I had a credit card, so I might have managed somehow, but I decided to accept the treat. I came this close to saying, *You can have my body as payment,* but I thought the joke would come dangerously close to trampling on his gentlemanly idealism, so I decided not to.

When we left the restaurant, the wind was cold. It was still winter, I thought, a little surprised.

So much had happened since last fall, I'd been feeling like it had been winter for a long time. After Dad died, I'd felt like I'd sat down on the ground and couldn't get up. Time had passed so quickly, it seemed impossible that my heart would ever catch up to it. But recently, my felt sense had finally been making up ground, and time seemed to be moving more slowly now. Living with Mom, who lived slowly on purpose, probably had a lot to do with it.

I briefly closed my eyes in the wind, and thought: *Mom won't be in my life forever. Even I'm going to disappear into this wind someday. Then we'll all just be skeletons fallen by the side of the road. No different from Dad.*

A premonition of the end that would come to me someday enveloped me softly.

It was neither uncomfortable nor miserable. I felt myself expanding, and I knew that where Dad was now wasn't so bad. It wasn't like I'd seen in that dream, narrow and constricting, and guarded by that woman. He'd been exposed to the elements, been taken apart, had expanded and scattered, and yet his center could still be sensed—that was the comforting impression I got from the vision.

"What shall we do?" Yamazaki-san said. "What time do you need to get home?"

"I don't want to be much later than midnight," I said.

"Of course, your mom would worry," he said.

I twined my arm around Yamazaki-san's sturdy arm. "I don't know why," I said, "Maybe because we prayed together. But I feel really easy around you. Like it's easy for me to be how I'm meant to be."

"My ex-wife used to tell me that, too," he said.

"I guess that's just what you're like, then," I said, and laughed. *What's more*, I was thinking, *when I'm with him, I feel like a woman.*

The concourse outside the station was crowded with buses and cars. Almost everyone was dressed in a suit. They filled the evening streets with the high spirits of people who'd had a drink or two.

"Why do you like me, and why do you want to do it with me?" Yamazaki-san said. "I know it's ridiculous to ask, and not suave at all, but I'd like to know."

He was the kind of person who liked things to have a reason, I thought, *some kind of through line.* There was a pleasant smell coming from his clothes, like fragrant roasted nuts. *And if something made sense to him, it wouldn't bother him one jot if it was generally frowned upon—like getting it on with your best friend's daughter, and when you knew her mother, too.* That was the impression I got from his question.

"This whole time since Dad died, the times when I've been with you have been the only times when my life had color. When I talked to you, those were the only times I wasn't worrying about someone else," I said.

I couldn't tell him that having sex with my boyfriend had

made me figure out that he was the one I really wanted to be doing it with, or that his voice had been the only thing that had given me hope to keep living. It would have been too disrespectful toward Shintani-kun, who'd taken the trouble to find me and get to know me.

"I'm sorry it sounds so childish," I said. "But it's true. And I'd been such a good girl these last couple of years—consoling Mom, going to the bistro every day, working hard, grieving properly, going to bed and getting up early, working some more . . . It was so far from what Dad had gone through, drifting and drifting until he met his death, it felt like I'd left something behind.

"It's not that I want to work off my frustrations by sleeping with someone I like, or that I want to find out how Dad might have felt by letting an older, more experienced man have his way with me, or that I have a secret crush on you and wish that we could be together. I just want to do something about my feelings, which are a mixture of all of these, to get them out into the real world."

"Okay, it's a deal," Yamazaki-san said. "Let's fuck."

"I can't believe you said that!" I said, and laughed.

I felt surprisingly calm. I must been felt confident that we were definitely connecting as man and woman, as people, over and beyond our roles.

We walked in silence. The last thing we'd said had been— "You don't mind coming back to mine?"—"I don't."

I kept hold of Yamazaki-san's hand the whole way so that the dream wouldn't end, the miracle wouldn't disappear

I texted Mom: *Feeling down after visiting the spot where Dad died, so I'm having a drink. Will be late back but don't worry, I'm not dwelling on things!*

I knew Mom wasn't that interested in my life, so I wasn't at all concerned about her finding out. I thought about how, for the next few hours, I was about to step out of the normal flow of my life, and that made me feel strangely elated. I wasn't alone, and I wasn't going into a lonesome shadow. My usual life, my responsibilities, my past, my relationships—I could just leave it all behind.

Dad's feelings must have weighed several hundred times more heavily on him, but I felt like I'd caught a glimpse of the tip of tail of what he must have felt. The sense of release was so violent I thought I might soar too high, and breathe in too much freedom, and burn myself up in the flames of my own emotions.

Yamazaki-san's place was on the fifth floor of a fancy, irregularly shaped apartment building. When he opened the door, the apartment was sparse and tidy, and a slinky gray cat appeared from inside.

"She left the cat," Yamazaki-san said.

"Maybe so it could keep you company," I said.

"No, she took it at first, but she brought it back again when the baby arrived, saying she couldn't keep it. We've both been abandoned," he said, stroking the cat.

I knew I might end up hurting him one day, and so he might me. But just then, I felt infinitely tender toward both of them—the cat, and Yamazaki-san.

"Coincidentally, we both happen to have bathed earlier, so let's say we can get straight to it," Yamazaki-san said.

"Coincidentally?" I said, and laughed.

Then we took each other's hand, and went to bed.

As we lay ourselves gently down, Yamazaki-san said, "There's a real possibility this might end up being the first and last time. But I'm serious about you, I swear."

I nodded, but when he said that I felt so sad, I had to cry.

This was different, I told myself. This wasn't like Dad and that woman, or me and Shintani-kun. There was no murkiness, no dead end here, even though I'd been looking for it, expecting it. There was too much that was clear and sure, and too much that led forward. Somehow, it was in no way at all what I'd hoped for.

Nothing was predictable, I thought.

Just as I hadn't been able to love Shintani-kun, even though he'd found me, and we were a good match in theory, and there was nothing about him I disliked—there wasn't a single thing in the world that I could know or decide in advance.

SEX WITH YAMAZAKI-SAN WAS different from sex with Shintani-kun. Shintani-kun's had been far more debauched, skillful, lascivious, and more pleasurable physically, which surprised me.

I must have sensed that, somehow, instinctively. I thought. *That was why I wanted to date him.*

But with Shintani-kun, there was nowhere to go. Where pleasure ended, so we'd have reached a dead end. There would be nothing more to see. Without realizing it, I'd already stood at the start of the path that had led Dad to his death, and seen down its length.

Yamazaki-san was clumsier, and somehow put me in mind of a middle schooler, but since he'd been married for a long time, he had the kind of gentleness which came from years of close intimacy with a woman, and I remembered his too-beautiful ex-wife and felt pained. My chest hurt so much, I didn't feel much pleasure or any elation at having betrayed Dad, or let Mom down.

But I felt so much tenderness for every movement he made that it made me shiver. I understood clearly, though not in words, that he was in the process of starting to really care for me. I felt certain he was seeing me as I really was.

Shintani-kun and Yamazaki-san had both given me things I'd wanted—the experience and physical compatibility, and the pure sexual pleasure of being with an older man; and the romance and considerate, awkward sex of a younger man—even though in my immaturity I'd been taken in by their appearances and confused one for the other. I felt like reality had somehow stepped in to sort out these elements that had long been muddled up inside me.

After a long while, when Yamazaki-san finally entered me, I had the sense that something conclusive had happened. There was no going back, and nor did I want to. I didn't have to worry about anything anymore—that was how it felt.

Whether he felt it, too, I didn't know.

This was something just for me, which I intended to keep safe for a very long time.

WE MUST HAVE BEEN tired from our trip, because both of us fell into a deep sleep for an hour or so.

When I opened my eyes again, the world looked different. I felt like everything had returned to its true form. The spell of love still held, and everything looked bright and hopeful.

The cat was asleep in a soft mass by my side, and beyond it was Yamazaki-san, who had been watching me sleep.

It was one thirty in the morning. It was time for me to go.

I sat up slowly and started to get dressed. I didn't want to leave, but I didn't have much choice. It was time for the spell to be broken.

"I was counting on feeling more self-loathing than this," Yamazaki-san said, frowning.

"I'm a grown woman now, I can take care of myself," I said.

"Don't speak, Yocchan," he said. "I'm trying to forget that you're Imo's daughter, Yocchan. I want to pretend you're just some young and attractive girl I picked up because I fancied her."

I thought about how I loved his knobbly knees, and even the hairs on his fingers.

"That's not going to happen," I said. "The fact you need to try gives it away." I stroked the cat, and smiled.

Yamazaki-san gave me a big hug outside his door, and we held hands and walked back to the main road together.

"We won't see each other for a while," he said. "Shit, I won't see you."

"When spring comes," I said. "I'll get in touch when I'm back from France. I'd like it if you felt able go to the aquarium with me, depending on how you feel then."

"Okay. Let's do that," he said.

"I have something to ask you," I said. Some tears fell from my eyes. How much more did I have to cry before my tears would run dry? I was tired of crying, tired from crying. And yet. "Please don't find someone else before spring. I don't mind if you sleep with people, but don't live with anyone," I said.

"I won't," he said, and stroked my head.

Like a father, and like a lover. Like both those things I was missing.

In the city, the midnight air was clear and cold. I breathed it in until it filled my lungs. I felt a longing for the heat that lingered in my body as the cold quickly stole it away.

I got into the taxi, and, as though it was a spell to make everything okay, said: "To Shimokitazawa, please."

It was my hometown for now; the place where I had something to protect; the place I was going home to.

The door swung closed and Yamazaki-san waved at me in the darkness. Then he turned around and went home, back into the room where we'd made love—definitely, certainly.

My heart felt so full I couldn't think properly, so I got out of the taxi by the station entrance on Chazawa-Dori.

Despite the late hour, the street was still busy, and I was overcome by memories of being with Shintani-kun. *I don't think trying to drown my sorrows in pleasures of the flesh is working for me right now,* I thought. *I guess I'll feel more curious about seeing pleasure through to its end once I'm Dad's age.*

There was so much I still didn't understand, I reflected. Dad and that woman—their relationship, what she'd been like, what they'd seen, anything: I hated to admit it, but all of it was theirs alone. I wanted to think they alone had staked their lives to see it. Then there was what had been Dad's alone, just as Mom and I had been precious to him.

No one could hold anything with you, but we could touch, and overlap, in ways that made us feel like we did.

Good-bye, Shintani-kun. And thanks.

That made me feel a little upset, but inside, I was still full of the warmth of Yamazaki-san's body. I cradled it gently, like a treasure, and walked through Azuma-Dori toward Osho.

The restaurant was lit up brightly, and full of noise and bustle, and people filling their bellies with pot stickers. It made me happy to see them through the glass.

I turned left and came back out onto Chazawa-Dori, and walked to where the bistro had been. The building was completely dark, but still standing.

Soon the lot would be empty again, and the cherry tree would be cut down. The life that had adorned the street at night with so much color and beauty would be gone. There was nothing I could do. I could thank the tree, but I wouldn't get a response. I touched its bark as I'd always done, but it only made me sadder to know we'd be parting soon. I could hardly believe it wasn't going to be here to bloom come spring.

The heavy wooden door that I'd pulled open every day would soon be no more. It seemed incredible. Yet the sight of it, and the weight of it, still remained inside me, surprisingly solid to the touch. This too was all mine, but also had been touched and shared by every person who walked through this town. It would never disappear, even if we all did.

They were a part of me just as much as the times that I'd spent with Dad, or his DNA.

Nothing could take away the sights that my eyes had seen, that my mind remembered, or that I lived in the very cells that made up my body. *Take that, time,* I thought, and squeezed my hand into a fist.

Under the freezing starry sky, I felt an understanding make its way deeper into me: the preciousness of me, as an individual, with my own experience which no one else in the world could know the whole of, but which I shared parts of with so many people everywhere whose experiences touched and overlapped with mine, even if I was young and miserable and looked like I had nothing at all.

I closed my eyes and saw the cherry tree in my mind's eye in full bloom, its branches laden with pale pink flowers swaying on the wind.

Beneath it, the Les Liens in my heart was open for business as usual, quietly, forever.

It was never going to disappear. It was safe.

I thought again, and resolved to see new sights and make new memories when spring came. Paris, the countryside in France, so many beautiful landscapes, good food, Michiyo-san's determined expression—all these things. And, just maybe, the way Yamazaki-san looked at different times, too—we might sometimes hate each other, or fight, or treat each other coldly, but I wasn't afraid, for now. Or we might not see each other again. That was for future me to think about once I was back from France. No one could tell how things might be by then, and the only way I could know who I would be at that point was by growing into that person, day by day, until we got there.

It wasn't just that I'd bedded someone I liked, someone I'd chosen. And it wasn't simply that I was in high spirits from having done what I needed to for Dad.

If someone had asked me how I'd spent this period in my life, I'd have said I'd done nothing in particular. It had all felt like a dream. But I drew confidence and satisfaction from the fact that I had in fact achieved things, that there had been a through line. Even when I'd felt suffocated and short of breath with nowhere to go, I'd done what I could, and it had all linked up and moved forward, and before I knew it I was coming up for breath somewhere where I was no longer weighed down. That place just happened to be here, tonight.

Right now, I seemed to be standing on my own in the middle of the night on a cold and lonely street, but when I thought of the wider town, I wasn't alone at all.

Just down the street, Chizuru-san would be at her bar, probably frying up a delicious snack. A little while ago, Eri-chan would have tidied the tea house to its usual serene state and quietly walked home across the street of shops on the east side. Hacchan, always the ladies' man, would have closed up at the used bookstore and gone out to see his date for the evening. The couple at the coffee roastery would have spent the day brewing and serving coffee, in their aprons and with their bandanas tied around their brows. Michiyo-san would probably be in touch tomorrow about arrangements for our trip. At this hour, Miyuki-san and Tecchan at the Thai restaurant might still be clearing up together after the evening's service. Soon they'd be going home, companionably, through the residential streets of the neighborhood.

My mind conjured up the faces and smiles and gestures of even more of the many people I'd met since coming to live and work in Shimokitazawa. No doubt the people Mom and I had come to know here had each spent another ordinary day of their lives in this town.

That was what a town was made of.

I could sense the daily movements and patterns of people I hadn't even known about few years ago coming in and out of this town like breath. I wasn't alone. There were other people, people I didn't know, coming in and out of this town, too, the same way, and all of that was how a town was made.

It was just as the pianist Fujiko Hemming had said. On first glance it looked chaotic, and muddy, and ugly, but when your eyes were open, you saw that all the movements and elements wove themselves into a wonderful pattern. What a joyful sight it was.

It was like a twining plant, made of a mixture of desire and worry and misery and love and splendid smiles and abundance and everything else in our collective unconscious. Even if the vine was severed with a hatchet, or burned to the ground, nothing would take away the landscapes inside people's hearts or the time that lived on inside them.

Through me, Dad was also now firmly a part of this realm.

That was what the town had shown me. *Thank you, Shimokitazawa. You wrapped me gently and let me rest and showed me what was true. No matter how you change, may you remain here forever, tenaciously sending up new shoots . . .*

I layered my voice with the many that had no doubt already expressed this simple wish.

Each day, I walked across this battlefield of remembrance—which was littered with the dead bodies of the hopes of those who had fallen victim to invisible powers, and those who had departed but left their hearts in this town—knowing that my footsteps left their mark on the ground like flowers offered in their memory.

The town I grew up in worked the same way. But the reason I only understood all this when I moved here was because this was a town where the wind blew through, and people loved it and cherished it especially.

I started walking again, and even though I was wearing grown-up shoes on a grown woman's feet, the lightness of my step felt just the same as they had when I'd walked in my favorite childhood sneakers, which Dad had taken me to buy.

Beyond these crossroads was my home, where my mother was waiting. I looked up at the light in the window of the room where she was. I saw the TV's big screen flashing light into the room. My father was gone now, but my mother was here. I could be with her today, for certain, at least, and hopefully much longer than that.

I'm coming home now, Mother—Mother, I'm glad you're here—I'll be coming through the door in a moment.

As I called out to her silently, I found myself holding something within me that could only be described as an enormous happiness, as though a star had fallen, twinkling, straight into my chest.

Nothing had changed. The clouds hadn't disappeared. But my heart was replete with something like an answer.

Afterword

■ ■ ■

WHEN MY LATE FATHER read this book, he called me on the phone to give me his long and rambling opinion about its pacing, and also how I seemed to have written it about my own father. I didn't know what to say. A newspaper serial always requires a certain amount of repetition and exposition, but more importantly, the dad in the story was a completely different type of dad than him.

But when I was reading the proofs for the paperback, not long after losing him so suddenly, I found the characters in the novel expressing my feelings so perfectly that I felt supported and reassured by my own novel. I even wondered whether I'd somehow known what I'd need.

I was going through a time where I couldn't find the answers I needed, no matter how much I thought or wondered or tried to guess, because the person who could tell me was gone. I was mired in heavy shadow. I spent my days with endless questions from which there was no real relief.

I even thought my father might have had a point.

People often criticize my work for being unrealistic and full of ideas that sound good, but which they wouldn't be able to keep believing in if they were faced with the death of a loved one. They also tell me that adults have various responsibilities and obligations that mean they can't live by just following their feelings as I do. But it turned out that actually, when I found myself in that situation, what I'd written felt very natural and even healing, so I felt confident that I hadn't been on the wrong track after all.

I had a ways to go before I reached a level where I could heal people who were very different from me, but anyone of an even slightly similar type I thought I could confidently say I could console. I thought I had gotten this far, at least.

It might sound all too optimistic, but that was what I thought.

THIS NOVEL GAVE ME the opportunity to forge a strong and ongoing relationship with the people at Mainichi Newspapers; I was able to deepen and cement my friendship with its illustrator Mai Ohno; I strengthened my links with the Pure Road Flea Market through organizing the small, handmade event which was going to be my last public appearance; I met and made a friend in Mamiko Ueyama, who helped us with it; and I became indebted to Hideyuki Hasunuma of One Love Books, who contributed so much to the event out of the goodness of his heart. I celebrated with many editors who came by despite it being published by a different publishing house, spent quality time with Ishihara-san and Tsuboi-san at Gentosha making the paperback, went on a research trip to Ibaraki and had a great time with Akashi Oumi and his wife—this novel has truly given me so much.

Although Les Liens, where the story is set, has closed, its chef Yoshizawa-san still serves up good food daily at Au Péché Gourmand, her new bistro in Hatagaya, which is always bustling. Her barley salad is still on the menu, and still tastes of life.

I can't list all your names here, since that would take an infinite amount of space, but I am so grateful to everyone who was involved in making this book, and every reader who read it, and every person who attended what was probably my last book signing ever. Thank you.

SADLY, THE NEIGHBORHOOD OF Shimokitazawa continues to become a lonelier place. Its wonderful independent shops are disappearing one after the other, being replaced by chain stores and hostess clubs. "Dr. Akahige," the street masseur, is nowhere to be seen. The mah-jong parlors that used to fill the streets with the sound of clicking tiles are no longer. Hamadako the *takoyaki* stall has closed, as has Cicouté Cafe.

I'm not trying to bemoan the passage of time, or say that change is wrong. Some things are probably inevitable, and since I grew up in the heyday of independent businesses, my fondness for them might be simple nostalgia.

But the way things are going, there will be less and less space for individuals to find their niche within a community, and less and less leeway for people to live at a pace that suits them. Customers will be forced to conform to the business's timetable, and learn to consume what they are given within the time they are allotted, like livestock. In that kind of situation there can be no opportunity for personal relationships to take root.

All I can do is to express my hope that the powers that resist this trend will somehow make it through, and that times will move again toward the better, so that businesses will once again be able to invest in things beyond money.

I recently went to the new Dover Street Market in Ginza set up by Comme des Garçons. Fewer people are investing in fashion now, and with times being hard, no doubt there are some ways in which they've been forced to cut costs. But I was moved by the belief and intent behind a domestic fashion house deciding to invest in culture in such a way at this juncture.

Some things are rewarding enough and meaningful enough that as humans, we choose to do them even if in purely financial terms it would be more profitable not to. My sense is that as long as we have bodies, our basic human desires will remain more or less the same. I only pray for the survival of all the many fine shops that still quietly continue to exist.

—Banana Yoshimoto